W9-BPM-659

even more
SHORT & SHIVERY

FORTY-FIVE CHILLING TALES

even more
SHORT & SHIVERY

Retold by
Robert D. San Souci

Illustrated by
Katherine Coville and Jacqueline Rogers

SCHOLASTIC INC.
New York Toronto London Auckland Sydney
Mexico City New Delhi Hong Kong

No part of this publication may be reproduced in whole or in part, or stored in a retrieval system, or transmitted in any form or by any means, electronic, mechanical, photocopying, recording, or otherwise without written permission of the publisher. For information regarding permission, write to Doubleday, a division of Bantam Doubleday Dell Publishing Group, Inc., Attention: Permissions Department, 1540 Broadway, New York, NY 10036.

ISBN 0-439-04233-X

Text copyright © 1987, 1994 by Robert D. San Souci.
Illustrations copyright © 1994 by Katherine Coville and Jacqueline Rogers.
Compilation copyright © 1998 by Scholastic Inc.
SCHOLASTIC and associated logos are trademarks and/or
registered trademarks of Scholastic, Inc.

12 11 10 9 8 7 6 5 4 3 2 1   8 9/9 0 1 2 3/0

Printed in the U.S.A.   40

First Scholastic printing, September 1998.

To my good friends Cherie and Larry Jung,
who also enjoy exploring the dark fantastic

Contents

Introduction

They're baaaaack! A fresh selection of "ghoulies and ghosties and long-leggety beasties"—and their cousins—from legends and folk tales all around the world.

Welcome, old friends and new, to this second collection of some of my favorite scary tales. I've had a chance to visit with young readers all around the country who have helped me decide what stories to include here. I am thankful to these friends in Alabama, California, Colorado, Delaware, Illinois, Kansas, Massachusetts, Michigan, Nebraska, Ohio, Oklahoma, Oregon, Washington, and elsewhere—this book is dedicated to all of you.

Many writers argue that a scary tale ought to be short. Now, I don't necessarily agree with this. Two novels that I first read in high school still chill me, though I've read each book more than a dozen times: *The Haunting of Hill House* by Shirley Jackson and *The House on the Borderland* by William Hope Hodgson.

But the short form can give a payoff as fast and powerful as a karate chop. Look at how the two shortest ghost stories in the world take just a few words to set up a situation, deliver a punch, and leave a lingering thrill in our imagination. The first "haunted room" tale runs in full:

He woke up frightened and reached for the matches, and the matches were put in his hand.

The "runner-up shorty" is called "The Men in the Turnip Field." It's very old, and it goes:

There was two fellows out working in a field, hoeing turnips they was, and the one he stop and he lean on his hoe, and he mop his face and he say, "Yur—I don't believe in these yur ghosteses!"

And t'other man he say, "Don't 'ee?"

*And he **vanished**!*

I hope you'll have as much fun discovering these shivery tales now, as I did finding them earlier, and retelling them. For those of you who want to know more about the background of individual stories, I have included a "Notes on Sources" at the end of this volume.

In the stories that follow you'll meet Bishop Hatto, who really had a problem with mice . . . Tom Walker, who should have read the not-so-fine print in his contract with the devil . . . and poor Odette, who finds a bundle that should not be unwrapped until Christmas—or ever! You'll also meet flying cannibal heads; vengeful elves and banshees; deadly forest spirits and goblins; and a curious creature that assembles itself out of bones and bits of other animals.

I hope you enjoy meeting them and their ghastly friends. Judging by the way they're grinning and rubbing their bony hands or paws or claws together, I'd say they're eager—just *dying*—to meet you!

even more
SHORT & SHIVERY

The Mouse Tower

(Germany)

In the middle of the Rhine River, near the city of Bingen, there has stood for hundreds of years a fortified rock topped by a large tower, called the *Mauseturm*, or mouse tower. Legend has long held that this was the scene of a terrible punishment sent by God upon a bishop who betrayed the faithful in his care.

In the year 970, Germany suffered from a terrible famine. In desperation, people were reduced to eating dogs and cats, and still countless numbers died of hunger. At this time, Hatto the Second was bishop of the region. Every day the starving poor would crowd around his door, begging for bread. It was widely known that he had plentiful supplies of grain set aside from the good harvest the year before.

But the bishop refused to part with the mounds of grain locked away in his bulging storehouses. His only thought was to increase his personal fortune.

From the high window of his palace, he would watch poor people fainting from hunger on the streets and storming the bread market, where they would take the bread by force. The bishop felt no pity at all for these starving people. But he soon grew weary of their cries day and night as they crowded around his palace walls, begging for a crust of bread, a handful of corn.

At last the bishop decided to quiet the mob. From his window he announced to them, "Let all you poor and needy gather in my great barn outside the city. There I shall feed you."

So it was that, from all directions, from near and far, a desperate army of hungry folk flocked to the bishop's barn. Loudly they sang the bishop's praises, while his soldiers urged them into the barn.

When the vast wooden structure could hold no more, the treacherous bishop ordered his soldiers to seal the doors. Then he had his men set fire to the barn, and burned the unfortunates, young and old, men and women. When the flames were at their highest, and the agonized cries were loudest, Hatto said, "Hear, hear, how the mice squeak! In faith, 'tis an excellent bonfire. The country is greatly obliged to me for ridding it of such mice who would only consume our precious corn."

The shouts and screams for mercy seemed to hang in the air long after the barn was reduced to nothing more than smoking embers.

Afterward, content with his day's work, the wicked man returned to his palace. There he sat down merrily to supper, and afterward slept the night like an innocent man.

But God soon saw to it that Bishop Hatto never slept again.

The very next morning, the bishop discovered his palace was infested with mice. They scurried down corridors and crawled over his feet while he took his ease or tried to read. They fouled the food in his larder and chewed his books and papers. They bit anyone who tried to drive them away. No efforts on his part could free Bishop Hatto from their torments.

When he entered his great hall, he discovered that mice had eaten his portrait out of its frame. The rectangle of splintered wood held only a few tatters of canvas. A short time later, a frightened farm servant reported to him that mice had devoured all the corn in his granaries.

Immediately thereafter, a second terrified messenger arrived and reported that a huge tide of mice was scurrying toward his palace.

Rushing to his window, the bishop could see the roads and fields dark with the advancing army. The vast horde of mice was chewing remorselessly through both hedge and wall, as the creatures made straight for the palace. The sound of their shrieking and squeaking chilled him to the heart.

Full of terror, Bishop Hatto escaped through the rear gate and commanded his men to row him out to his tower in the middle of the Rhine River. There he ordered his servants to bar every entrance.

But the mice followed him. They swam across the river, clambered up the rock, and crawled through every crack and crevice of the battlements. Swarming over the tower, they chewed their way in by the thousands, through oaken doors and plank floors and wooden ceilings.

And when they had cornered the wicked bishop, they climbed, dropped, and leaped upon him from all sides. As one old poem has it:

> They whetted their teeth against the stones,
> And then they picked the bishop's bones;
> They gnawed the flesh from every limb,
> For they were sent to punish him.

Then, as suddenly as they had appeared, the swarms of mice disappeared. Many people were convinced that the

animals were really the souls of those the bishop had so cruelly slain. The *Mauseturm* remains a place of fearful fascination. It is rumored that one can still hear the ghostly cries of the wretched bishop and the chittering of hordes of unseen mice on the anniversary of the fatal barn fire.

The Devil and
Tom Walker

(United States—from a tale by Washington Irving)

A few miles from Boston, the sea has cut a deep inlet that winds several miles inland and ends in a thickly wooded swamp. On one side of the water is a dark grove of trees; on the opposite side the land rises abruptly from the shore into a high ridge, on which grow scattered oaks of immense age and size. Under one such tree, according to old stories, Captain Kidd the pirate buried a great treasure. The stories add that the devil oversaw the hiding of the money, and took it under his guardianship, as he always does with buried treasure that has been ill-gotten. Kidd never returned to claim his gold, being captured soon after at Boston, sent to England, and there hanged for piracy.

Later, in the year 1727, a miserly fellow named Tom Walker dwelled near this place. He lived in a forlorn house surrounded by a few straggling trees. One day Tom took a shortcut homeward, through the swamp. Like most shortcuts, it was an ill-chosen route.

It was dusk when Tom reached the ruins of an old fort in the middle of the swamp. He paused to rest on the trunk of a fallen hemlock. Absently, he turned up the soil with his walking staff. Suddenly his staff struck something hard, and he uncovered an ancient skull with a tomahawk buried deep in it.

"Humph!" said Tom Walker as he gave it a kick.

"Let that skull alone!" said a gruff voice. Tom looked up and saw a tall man dressed in black seated opposite him on the stump of a tree. He scowled at Tom with a pair of large red eyes. "What are you doing on my ground?"

"And pray, who are you, if I may be so bold?" said Tom.

"Oh, I go by various names. In this neighborhood I am known by the name of The Black Woodsman."

"If I mistake not," said Tom sturdily, "you are also commonly called Old Scratch."

"At your service!" replied the devil with a nod.

And so the two began a conversation as Tom returned homeward. The dark man told him of huge sums of gold and silver buried by Kidd the pirate, under the oak trees on the high ridge. This treasure was protected by his power, so that only someone who gained his favor could find it. This he offered to Tom, on certain conditions.

The conditions must have been very hard, because Tom asked for time to think about them, and he was not a man to worry about trifles when money was in view. When they reached the edge of the swamp, Tom said, "What proof have I that all you have been telling me is true?"

"Here's my signature," said Old Scratch, pressing his finger against Tom's forehead. Then he turned off into the swamp, and seemed to go down, down, down into the earth, until he totally disappeared.

When Tom reached home, he found a black fingerprint, which nothing could erase, on his forehead. This made him think even more carefully about the terms he had been offered.

Soon enough, however, greed won over caution. One evening Tom set out for the abandoned fort. Soon he met The Black Woodsman, with his ax on his shoulder, strolling through the swamp, humming a tune. By degrees Tom brought up the subject of business, and they began to

7

haggle about the terms on which Tom was to have the pirate's treasure.

"You shall become a moneylender," the devil proposed. "You shall open a shop in Boston. You shall lend money to the desperate at ruinous rates, extort bonds, foreclose mortgages, and drive the merchants to bankruptcy—"

"I'll drive them to the devil!" cried Tom.

"Exactly," said the man in black with a grim smile. Then he extended his hand, saying, "Done!"

"Done!" said Tom Walker.

So they shook hands and struck a bargain.

Soon Tom Walker was seated behind his new desk in a countinghouse in Boston. The place was richly furnished, and had been paid for in antique gold coins to which traces of dark earth still clung.

His business was thronged by the needy who hoped to keep a roof over their heads and bread on the table; the foolhardy who dreamed of turning borrowed money into great fortunes; gamblers whose luck had run out; and merchants whose credit had dried up. In short, everyone driven to raise money by desperate means and desperate sacrifices hurried to Tom Walker.

Tom acted like a friend, but he always demanded full return and more for the money he loaned. He squeezed his customers as dry as a sponge, and sent them away destitute. In this way he became a rich and mighty man, and built himself a vast house.

As Tom grew old, however, he grew thoughtful. Having secured the good things of this world, he began to worry about the next. He regretted his deal with the devil, and tried to think of how to escape from his bargain with The Black Woodsman. All of a sudden he became a violent

churchgoer. He prayed loudly, as if he could take possession of heaven by the force of lungs. He constantly cen-
sured his neighbors, and seemed to think that every sin he
noted in them was a credit to him. Soon his zeal became as
notorious as his riches.

In spite of all this, Tom dreaded that the devil would
have his due after all and carry him off. So Tom always
kept a small Bible in his coat pocket. He also had a huge
Bible on his countinghouse desk, and was frequently
found reading the Bible when people called on business.
Then he would lay his spectacles in the book to mark the
place, while he drove some ruinous bargain.

One hot summer afternoon, as a black thunderstorm
was coming up, Tom sat in his countinghouse in his white
cap and silk robe. He was about to foreclose a mortgage,
which would ruin an unlucky man.

"My family will be driven to the poorhouse," the
wretched man pleaded.

"I must take care of myself," replied Tom.

"But you have made so much money out of me already!" the other cried.

Tom lost his patience and his piety. "The devil take me,"
said he, "if I have made a farthing!"

Just then, there were three loud knocks at the door.
Tom opened it to see who was there. A man dressed in a
black woodsman's outfit was holding a black horse, which
neighed and stamped with impatience.

"Tom, you're come for," said the fellow gruffly. Tom
shrank back, but too late. He had left his little Bible in his
coat pocket, and his big Bible on the desk, under the
mortgage he was about to foreclose. Never was a sinner
taken more unawares.

The black figure whisked him into the saddle, and the

horse galloped away down the streets. Tom Walker's white cap bobbed up and down, his robe fluttered in the wind, and the steed struck fire out of the cobblestones at every bound. The dark woodsman disappeared in a blaze of black fire.

Tom never returned to foreclose the mortgage. A man who lived on the border of the swamp reported that at the height of the thunderstorm he had heard a great clattering of hoofs and a howling along the road. He ran to the window and caught sight of a figure on a horse that raced like mad across the fields and down into the black swamp toward the old fort. Shortly thereafter, a lightning bolt fell and seemed to set the whole forest ablaze.

When neighbors searched Tom's offices they found all his bonds and mortgages burned to cinders. His huge iron chest was filled with chips and shavings of wood instead of gold and silver. The next day his house caught fire and burned to the ground.

Such was the end of Tom Walker and his ill-gotten wealth.

The Greedy Daughter

(Italy)

There once was a widow who had a daughter who was so greedy that the poor woman did not know what to do with her. She would gobble up everything in the house. When the widow came home from selling flowers in the market square, she would find nothing left to eat.

Now it happened that they had a wolf as a neighbor. The wolf had a frying pan, while the girl's mother was too poor to own one. Whenever she wanted to fry something, the mother sent her daughter, Filomena, to borrow the wolf's frying pan.

The wolf was very glad to loan the skillet to the widow. And he always sent a nice omelette in it so it would not be empty. The wolf intended this omelette for both mother and daughter. But Filomena was so greedy and so selfish that she always ate the omelette on the way home. Her poor mother never had so much as a taste.

When the good woman was finished with her frying, she would say to her daughter, "Filomena, in the morning scour the pan clean and return it to our neighbor. Take with you a loaf of the bread I baked today to thank him."

Filomena was lazy as well as greedy. She refused to clean the greasy frying pan. She waited until her mother had gone to the market square. Then she ate the loaf of

11

bread meant for the wolf. After this, she took some mud, baked it in the fireplace, and put it in the frying pan. "Our neighbor is only a wolf, after all," she said to herself. "He will not know baked dirt from good bread."

The wolf was hurt when he saw the earthen loaf, but he was too good-hearted to say anything. After Filomena was gone, he said to himself, "Well, well! Perhaps things are going so badly for the widow that she can offer me no more than a bit of baked mud and ash. Next time they borrow the frying pan, I will make them an even finer omelette."

Soon enough, the old woman asked Filomena to visit the wolf and beg for the loan of his skillet. This time the wolf gave the girl the pan with an omelette so light and filled with fine herbs and cheese and ham that the greedy girl got only a short distance from the wolf's house before she gobbled up every bit of it. Not a speck was left for her mother that evening.

When the widow had finished her frying, she said to Filomena, "In the morning, scrub out the skillet and return it. And take with you this pitcher of cream to thank our neighbor."

As soon as her mother had left the next morning, greedy Filomena drank down every drop of the cream. Then she took the empty pitcher and the greasy frying pan with her and walked to the wolf's house. She paused on the way to dip up a pitcherful of ditch water, muttering, "Why waste sweet cream on a wolf? This will serve quite as well."

Again the wolf was offended by the sight of the greasy pan and the pitcher of ditch water. But he thanked the unkind girl anyway. To himself, he said, "Now things must really be desperate in the poor woman's house, that she can only send common ditch water by way of thanks."

Then he set to scouring the pan himself.

It chanced soon after this that the wolf met the widow in the market square. "How are things with you?" he asked.

"Well enough," she said.

"How do you like my omelettes?" asked the wolf.

"I am sure you make delicious omelettes," replied the confused woman. "But I have never had the pleasure of tasting so much as a mouthful."

"Never tasted them!" exclaimed the wolf. "How many times have you sent Filomena to borrow my frying pan?"

"I am ashamed to say how many times," said the flustered woman. "A great many, certainly."

"And every time I sent you an omelette in it," the wolf said.

"Never a bit of one reached me," the woman confessed.

"Then that greedy girl of yours must have eaten them on the way home every time."

Now the poor mother, anxious to keep the wolf from being angry at her daughter, made all manner of excuses for Filomena's greediness. But the wolf had grown even more suspicious, so he said, "The omelettes would have been better had the frying pan been properly cleaned before it was sent back to me."

"Surely you are mistaken!" cried the widow. "Filomena told me herself that she always cleaned it inside and out, until it sparkled as bright as new silver." Then, worried because the wolf was growing angrier by the minute, the good woman said, "I hope you enjoyed the little gifts of bread and cream I sent to you."

"Dirty ash and ditch water are all your wretched child brought to me!" cried the wolf.

"Dear neighbor, surely you are joking!" said the worried woman. "Perhaps I burned the bread myself. If there was water in the cream, then the farmer I bought it from was a cheat."

"Oh, I know who has been the cheat," said the wolf. "Now I must be on my way. Farewell."

So saying, he hurried away.

But he did not return to his own home. Instead he raced to the woman's house.

When Filomena saw the angry wolf approaching, she slammed shut the door. Then she called out, "Why have you come here?"

"I'm here to punish you for your unkind gifts of dirt and ditch water," he roared, "and your greedy way with the omelettes entrusted to you and the bread and cream that were meant for me!"

"Surely," the wicked girl cried out, "if anything is amiss, it was my mother's doing. She is in the market square. Go and gobble up that good-for-nothing if you must."

The wolf just growled and broke down the door. The frightened girl scrambled under the bed to hide herself, but it was as easy for the wolf to go under the bed as to get anywhere else. So under he went, and dragged her out, and gobbled her down on the spot.

And that was the end of the greedy daughter.

The Pirate

(United States—adapted from a poem by Richard H. Dana)

Near the close of the eighteenth century, a ship lay in a Spanish port, being outfitted for a voyage to America. One day, a Spanish doña, a widow, came to the dock, seeking passage to America. The unfortunate woman had no way of knowing that Captain Lee, grown weary of the poverty that dogged his life, had turned pirate.

Eyeing her fine dress, her golden rings, and her jewels, Lee offered her false sympathy for the loss of her husband and falser promises of a swift, safe passage across the ocean. Charmed by the captain's manner, the woman put herself, her servants, and all her wealth in the buccaneer's grasp.

At the very last moment—just before the ship set sail—the *señora* had her most prized possession brought on board: a milk-white Arabian horse. The stallion was tethered on deck. But from the first it stamped and reared and whinnied as though it sensed the danger hiding behind the captain's polite words and gracious manner.

As soon as the ship was out of sight of land, the crew, at a signal from Lee, slew all the lady's attendants as they slept. Then he and his men forced the door of her cabin open. It fell inward with a crash, but the lady fought the pirate with all her strength. She managed to break free of Lee's grasp and fled to the deck of the ship.

There, she tried to untie the Arabian as it raged against the ropes that kept it captive. Realizing that she could not free the horse in time, the brave woman drew her dagger and climbed onto the railing. Calling down the vengeance of heaven on the pirate who had betrayed her, she swore to battle to the end. Lee, tiring of the game, signaled one of his men to stun the frantic woman with a belaying pin, and take her prisoner. But in the confusion, the stricken woman fell backward, into the sea, with a dreadful shriek.

At the sound, the horse snapped its bonds and charged around the deck, trampling many of the pirate's men underhoof. Firing twice with his long-barreled pistols, Lee dropped the Arabian to its knees. Then he had his men throw the still-living horse into the sea.

For a time the stallion seemed almost to ride the swelling waves. Then it gave a cry unlike any heard by mortal men before. It rang out over the wide waters, causing even the fiercest pirate to shiver. Lee clasped his hands to the sides of his head and prayed he would never hear such a sound again.

For a time the cries continued, but they grew fainter as the milk-white steed was carried farther and farther away by the waves. After a while they blended with the cries of the ever-present gulls, and the pirate captain's moment of fear passed.

Then Lee divided up the *señora*'s gold. Several fights broke out over the division of the booty. "Avast!" Lee roared. "I'll have no more fighting on my ship!" He pitched one of his men overboard as a warning to the others. An uneasy quiet followed, for the men knew their captain would toss anyone who defied his orders to the sharks.

When they neared Block Island, off the coast of Rhode Island, Lee decided that his ship was too well known in the coastal waters of America. With the *señora*'s gold loaded into a lifeboat, he ordered the ship abandoned and set on fire. Then he and his surviving cutthroats rowed to shore. There they silenced any suspicious locals with a little extra gold.

Soon all but Lee drifted away to other ports and pursuits. With his stolen fortune, Lee no longer felt he needed the life of a pirate. He became a wealthy merchant, and began to woo the daughter of the town judge.

Exactly one year from the night when he had hurled a torch into the rigging of his pirate ship and rowed toward a new life with his stolen gold, Lee was walking along the shore toward his lady's house on the edge of town. Suddenly a glare lit up the sea, and he froze in midstride. Even more chilling was the unearthly cry that issued from the brightness—a cry Lee had heard only once before and had hoped he would never hear again.

The light on the horizon rapidly grew until it was the size of a rising moon, shooting streamers of milk-white and blood-red light across the waves. Now the man could see that it came from a ship, all on fire. Her hull was ablaze; each mast was a pillar of fire; her sails were sheets of flame. She raced shoreward with uncanny speed.

But faster yet came a ghastly white shape: a spectral horse's head rising from the depths. In an instant, the milk-white stallion had emerged from the water. It galloped from wave to wave as though it were crossing land. A moment later it reached the shore, and sped like the wind across the sand to where the hapless Lee stood watching in horror. Never once did the burning eyes— like twin coals in the beast's head—leave Lee's own.

When it was only a few paces from him, the horse stopped, snorting and stamping the ground impatiently. A power he could not resist forced Lee to mount the dreadful steed. The moment he was astride the devil horse, the creature carried him to the highest cliff of the island.

From here Lee could clearly see not only the burning ship, but also, in the water tinted white and red by the ghostly blaze, he could make out the bodies of all those he had slain. They rose from the depths, their arms outstretched to him, beckoning him into their midst. Clearest of all was the image of the wretched *señora*, whose pale, waterlogged skirts seemed to melt into the waves upon which she walked. She pointed her finger at him and smiled a grim smile that turned his insides to ice.

"Have mercy, I beg you!" cried the former pirate.

But the horse shook its head as if it understood his plea. To his horror, Lee saw there was no mercy in the faces of his ghostly victims. With a shudder, he remembered that he had not shown any one of them mercy. All around, the night was filled with their calls: "Join us, join us, join us."

But more terrifying yet was the *señora*. As if his fright were some vast joke, she threw back her head and laughed. At first the sound was as shrill as a seagull's call—but it quickly deepened until it became as loud as the howl of gale winds that would tear a ship apart on the open sea.

Then the ghostly woman made a single gesture with her hand and vanished in a spout of flame.

Suddenly the specter horse leaped into the air and plunged down through the night air as if it were a steep slope. Across the sand it galloped while Lee twisted and cried out in wild despair.

But he was bound to the horse by some fearful spell. Soon the steed was racing across the water lit by the burning ship. All around Lee, half-submerged figures clawed at his boots and clutched at the tails of his coat.

On and on the demon horse rode, until the fiery hull

18

rose before Lee like a curtain of flame. With an anguished cry, he flung his arms over his eyes.

There was a final burst of twining red and white flame that lit the sea from one end of the island to the other. Then horse and rider, ship and ghosts vanished—extinguished as suddenly as a candle flame.

There was only an expanse of shadow-dark waves rolling endlessly, endlessly shoreward.

The Golden Arm

(British Isles—England)

There was once a handsome but miserly man who traveled far and wide in search of a wife. He cared little that a woman was young or old, pretty or plain, sweet-tempered or shrewish—he only insisted that she be rich, not poor.

At last he found a beautiful woman who was raven-haired, blue-eyed, and rosy-cheeked, with lips as full and ripe as cherries. She had been born without a right arm; but her father was so rich, he had had the finest goldsmith in England fashion her an arm of gold. It was this and her own fortune that made the miser decide to marry her. In truth, he was fonder of her golden arm than of all his wife's other gifts combined.

At first the young woman was in love with her husband, and dreamed that her good nature would sweeten his sour disposition. But his greed and miserliness soon turned her as sharp and bitter as himself. They spent long days and longer nights arguing. Whenever it seemed that she might go away and leave him, he would stroke her cheek, pat her golden arm, and promise to mend his pinchpenny ways.

But he never did. Again and again she would threaten to leave, but she never did. As time went on, the man grew even more tightfisted with their money.

In the depth of winter, his shivering wife said,

> *We have no wood,*
> *We lack for coals:*
> *Outside the winds howl like lost souls.*
> *Husband, dear, I beg you, please,*
> *Let me buy fuel before we freeze.*

But he answered,

> *Wood and coal cost more each day.*
> *I will not pay and pay and pay,*
> *And so throw all my wealth away.*
> *Not one penny will you get today.*

When their underfed horse no longer had the strength to pull their ancient carriage, his wife pleaded,

> *Our starving horse*
> *Is skin and bone.*
> *Our greaseless carriage wheels groan.*
> *Husband, dear, I beg you, please,*
> *Let me buy some oats and grease.*

But all he would say was,

> *Oats and grease cost more each day.*
> *I will not pay and pay and pay,*
> *And so throw all my wealth away.*
> *Not one penny will you get today.*

They had no food in the larder, and hunger made the poor woman frantic. She begged,

> *Our tea is weak,*
> *Our soup is thin,*

We live on crusts and turnip skins.
Husband, dear, I beg you, please,
Let me buy some meat and cheese.

But his answer was always the same,

Meat and cheese cost more each day.
I will not pay and pay and pay,
And so throw all my wealth away.
Not one penny will you get today.

Soon his wife grew sickly from lack of food and from loneliness. She would sit by the cold hearth, the fingers of her hand of flesh twined around the fingers of her golden hand, listening to the wind whistle up and down the chimney.

Her husband often sat beside her, just as silent, his eyes drawn always to the golden arm, which seemed to grow more beautiful every day, while her other arm wasted away.

Finally she took to her bed, knowing she would not rise from it again. Her husband sat beside her, stroking the golden arm, while she said:

Husband, as my last request,
I charge you: See that I shall rest
For all eternity
In the gown I wore as bride
With my golden arm beside,
Then shall I slumber peacefully.

He nodded and patted her golden arm. Then she sighed and closed her eyes a final time.

.   .   .

After she was dead, her husband put on his tall black hat and long black coat, and even managed to have a few tears in his eyes when he met his wife's family at her funeral. When she was laid to rest in the churchyard, he wept as though his heart were broken.

But as soon as the other mourners were gone, in the dead of night, he returned to the churchyard. There he dug up his wife's coffin and took her golden arm. Then he hurried home with his ghastly treasure, certain that no one would ever know what he had done.

To keep the golden arm safe from thieves, he hid it under his bed pillows. For two nights he fell asleep, dreaming dreams of golden kingdoms.

But on the third night, just as he was drifting into sleep, he suddenly woke up, thinking he had heard footsteps on the staircase.

> *I locked the door with special care,*
> *Surely there is no one there,*

he told himself as he drew the covers up to his chest.

He heard the sound again, a step or two higher.

> *That's just a mouse upon the stair,*
> *Surely there is no one there.*

But he drew the bedclothes up to his chin all the same.

A third time he heard the sound.

> *A drape was moved by restless air—*
> *Surely there is no one there,*

he whispered. Then he drew the blankets up to his nose.

One more time he heard the faint sound of a footstep; now it was just outside the door to his room.

Mustering all his courage, he said aloud,

> *I have no reason to beware:*
> *And yet I must know,* Who is there?

At these words, the ghost of his dead wife glided into the room. She stood at the foot of the bed and stared at him reproachfully.

Pretending not to be afraid, he spoke to the ghost, saying, "Your raven hair's grown lank and gray."

She answered, "The grave has stolen its sheen away."

"Your hollow eyes brim with dismay."

"The grave has stolen my joy away."

"Your cheeks are marked by sad decay."

"The grave has stolen their bloom away."

"Your gown is stained with moss and clay."

"The grave has stolen its beauty away."

"Why have you left your grave this day?"

"To fetch my arm you stole away!"

At this, the man cried out, and backed away from the ghost, as deep into the pillows on his bed as he could. But before he could deny the theft, he felt fingers—hard as steel, cold as the grave—wrap around his throat.

In a moment there was only silence.

In another moment,

> *There was a footfall on the stair,*
> *A gleam of gold,*
> *Then nothing there.*

The Serpent Woman

(Spain)

Long ago, in Spain, near the city of Cordova, there dwelled a man named Don Juan de Amarillo. Though he was far from young himself, he had a handsome young wife, Doña Pepa. No one knew where she came from: All anyone knew was that Don Juan had gone traveling for many years, and had returned with a new wife.

There was something uncanny about her perfect features, dark eyes, and skin as pale as marble and as cool to the touch. Her tall, thin form was strangely flexible and lithe. Though all Don Juan's friends were charmed by her beauty and elegant manners at first, they soon went out of their way to avoid the lady.

There was a *strangeness* about her. When pleased, she swayed her body to and fro with delight. If she was displeased, her head seemed to flatten out, and the touch of her hand was like a bite. She delighted in spreading gossip about her neighbors, whether they had offended her or not.

To all appearances, Don Juan adored his wife. But the servants whispered that they argued from morning to night, and that Don Juan seemed deathly afraid of Doña Pepa—especially when her head flattened in anger. Stories circulated that she was a sorceress who had bewitched the unhappy Don Juan.

Because Don Juan and his wife had no children, the old man decided to leave his wealth to his poor nephew, Don Luis, of whom he was very fond. He invited the young man to come from Aragon for a visit.

Don Luis was an honest, open-hearted young man who quickly became popular with his uncle's servants and friends. Only Doña Pepa disliked him. She seemed disgusted that people should discover that Don Juan had such poor relations.

Whenever she saw the young man, she would smile politely if anyone was watching. But when only he could see, she would shoot him a look of such scorn and hatred that he shuddered. At such moments her head flattened, her eyes grew long and narrow, and she moistened her lips (white with rage) with a hissing sound.

Don Luis lived in constant fear of her, and kept out of her way by every polite means. But she would not let him escape, and always revealed a little more of her hatred to him. He was sure that she hoped to drive him away from his uncle's house and his inheritance. Yet, for love of the kind Don Juan, the young man said nothing.

One night, returning from a visit to a friend, Don Luis lit a candle and headed toward his room. As he walked down the hall, he stumbled over what he thought was a coil of rope. To his horror, the rope uncoiled itself, and a large black snake glided upstairs and disappeared under his uncle's door.

Fearing for Don Juan, he pounded on the door until his uncle opened it and demanded crossly, "Why do you disturb my sleep in the middle of the night?"

"I saw a large black snake creep under your door, my dear uncle," the young man hastily explained.

"Nonsense!" exclaimed Don Juan, turning pale. "There is no serpent here."

"I insist on searching your room," said Don Luis.

"Very well," said his uncle, "but be quick about it."

Don Luis searched everywhere but found nothing. He was so quiet that he did not awaken Doña Pepa, who slept on until the moment he was leaving. Then she suddenly opened her eyes; her head flattened, and her eyes grew long and narrow. The young man quickly left the room with many apologies, but his dreams that night were filled with loathsome snakes.

The next morning, Don Luis found only his aunt when he went down to breakfast.

Doña Pepa stared at him coldly. "I warn you, nephew, you do not belong here," she said. "If you stay, I will teach you the true meaning of fear."

As she said this, she seized him by the wrist. He felt a stinging pain. He threw her hand aside and hurried out. But by the afternoon his arm had begun to swell and throb, until he had to go to the doctor in town.

The doctor examined his arm, noted a wound on his wrist, and said, "That is a serpent's bite."

"No," said Don Luis, "my aunt grabbed my arm in anger."

"I can give you medicine for the bite," said the doctor, who had met Doña Pepa many times. "For the rest, you will have to decide your own course of action."

The two men shared a glance of deep understanding.

That night, as Don Luis climbed into bed, he found the black snake coiled by his feet. Instantly he drew his sword and struck the reptile, cutting off a piece of its tail. The snake reared its head and bared its fangs, preparing to strike. But Don Luis slashed another piece off the tail. Hissing, the snake flowed to the door, then under it.

Don Luis followed it upstairs and saw it disappear under Don Juan's door. Don Luis did not alarm his uncle this time. He decided that the snake had a hiding hole in the wall or floor of the room and would remain hidden from any searchers.

The next morning, Doña Pepa did not appear. "Your aunt has a habit of sleepwalking," Don Juan explained to his nephew. "Last night she stepped on something sharp."

For days, Don Luis did not see his aunt. When she reappeared, she greeted him politely enough, but he noticed that she walked with a limp.

That night, Don Luis was surprised by the snake, which had hidden in a corner of his room. Only his quick reflexes saved him. He spun away from the deadly jaws, grabbed his sword, and struck the creature a few inches below its head. The wounded snake escaped before he could strike it again. When he looked down the hallway, he could see no trace of the thing. But he was sure that it had fled to its secret hiding place in his uncle's room.

For a month afterward, Doña Pepa kept to her darkened room. His uncle explained that she had fallen victim to a fever that required her to rest and avoid all company. At last, looking paler than ever, she appeared and accompanied Don Juan on an errand to Cordova. As she passed Don Luis, her dark eyes flashed with such hatred that he felt it like a blow.

When they were gone, he began a search of their room, determined to find out the secret of the black snake. He looked everywhere, but found nothing. Then, in a chest under a window, he discovered a skin striped like a serpent's. He guessed that the snake had hidden in the chest long enough to shed its skin.

Don Luis was taking the unwholesome thing downstairs when he heard his uncle's carriage returning. Since it was evening, the great fire in the main hall was burning. Without a thought, the young man threw the skin on the fire. It blazed, then quickly crisped and curled into nothing.

Suddenly there was a great commotion at the front door. Servants ran to and fro as Don Juan came in, carrying Doña Pepa, who had fainted. They set her on a couch, where she lay looking very pale and ill. A man was sent to fetch the doctor.

"What happened, dear uncle?" asked Don Luis.

"I don't know, I don't know," his uncle answered. "We had just stepped from the carriage when your aunt suddenly screamed that her skin was on fire. She began to twist about and beat her hands upon her skirt as though it were in flames. A moment later, she fell into my arms."

Don Luis glanced at the fireplace, where not a trace of the snakeskin remained. He remembered his mother telling him, when he was a child, "God sometimes punishes an evil woman by making her become a snake every night for a number of years equal to her crimes."

His thoughts were interrupted when the doctor arrived. He rushed to Doña Pepa's side, took up her hand, and felt for her pulse.

"What is the matter with her?" asked Don Luis.

"She is dead," replied the doctor.

Though Don Juan was genuinely saddened by his wife's untimely death, it seemed to his nephew that a burden of worries had dropped from him. His uncle's friends, arriving to offer comfort, commented that they had not seen the old man looking so well in years.

For a time, Don Luis concerned himself with setting his uncle's affairs in order. He began to think that his aunt's death at the moment he burned the snakeskin was merely an unhappy coincidence.

Then one morning the old woman who was his uncle's most trusted servant confided in Don Luis. "You know, señor, I prepared Doña Pepa for burial. While I was busy at my sad work, I saw the figure of a large snake traced upon the length of her body. Was that not strange?"

"Indeed," said Don Luis. "My aunt, God give her rest, took many secrets with her to the grave. And that, I think, is best for all of us."

Loft the Enchanter

(Iceland)

In the Middle Ages there was a boy named Loft, who chose to study magic, learning certain small spells and charms from a hermit who lived in the wilderness a distance from the village. It was rumored that the man had once been a great sorcerer but had lost most of his skill—and his senses—when he probed too deeply into the shadowy world of magic.

"Have a care, Loft," his neighbors warned, "or thou wilt suffer the same fate. Or a worse one!"

But the young man only laughed at them. "I will become the greatest wizard of all," he boasted. "I will hold the most powerful spirits in my hands."

When the good pastor of the village urged him to change his ways, Loft grew angry. He caused a monstrous shape to appear and frighten the pastor's horse while he was crossing a stream swollen with snowmelt. The pastor was tumbled into the raging water and barely escaped with his life. Thereafter, the clergyman offered prayers for Loft's soul but stayed out of his path.

In time, Loft traveled far to the north, where the most powerful sorcerers in the region kept a school for the study of the black arts. There he increased his skills and learned the dangerous secrets of the terrible book called *Greyskin*. In this, the greatest wizards and warlocks of the past had written down many of their most potent spells.

His unceasing pursuit of dark secrets turned his mind to wickedness. While he was still a student he punished a fellow student, a bully who had beaten him. Using magic, Loft created a doorway in a solid wall. From within came elfin music and sweet singing. When the curious boy stepped through it, the wall flowed back together, trapping him forever in the stone. The mystery of his disappearance caused great puzzlement, and more than a little suspicion was cast on Loft. But the young man denied any knowledge of the missing pupil's whereabouts.

Greedy for even more knowledge and power, Loft vowed to conjure up the ghost of the mightiest sorcerer of old, Gottskalk the Cruel. He hoped to compel that spirit to hand over the legendary book *Redskin*, which had been buried with the magician in his secret grave. In this book Gottskalk had gathered the most fearsome spells of old.

On a moonlit night, Loft barred the door to his tower room and began the conjuring spell. But as soon as he started, a voice moaned, "Cease, while there is still time."

"I will not," Loft answered boldly. He continued about his evil business.

A second time the voice warned, "Cease! There is but a little time to save yourself."

"Silence!" Loft commanded.

When Loft had fully cast his spell, the ghost of Gottskalk appeared. The figure was tall and lean, with burning eyes and skin as gray as the grave.

"Thou hast chanted well enough," said the spirit, "for all that thou didst stumble over certain words."

"I command thee, hand over the book *Redskin*," ordered Loft.

"Upstart," growled the specter. "Dost thou dare to treat me like some mere apprentice? Though thou study for a hundred times a hundred years, thou shalt never force me to surrender *Redskin* to thee."

"Give it here," Loft persisted, extending his hand. "As I have summoned thee, thou must do my bidding."

By the flickering candlelight, the ghost began to grow huge until it bent double at the ceiling. "Arrogant fool," the monstrous shape said with a laugh, "thy doom is sealed, because thou hast tampered with power thou cannot begin to understand."

Then the ghost began to laugh again. The sound was so loud that Loft pressed his hands to his ears. All the while, the vast gray figure continued to grow and swell, until it filled the room and forced Loft out onto the stairway landing.

Standing upright, the ghastly giant pressed its shoulders against the ceiling beams. The wood snapped and masonry rained down as it lifted the roof off the tower.

Loft fled, but the booming laughter followed him down the winding stairs. Suddenly a great foot thrust down through the overhead wreckage and tried to smash him like a bug. Loft threw himself out of the way, tumbling down the remaining steps and landing, bruised and dazed, at the bottom.

He forced himself to his feet, while the whole tower around him heaved and shook as in an earthquake. Walls cracked and falling dust nearly blinded him. From outside he could hear alarms and the cries of masters and students.

Loft stumbled to the stable, saddled his horse, and fled the sorcerers' school. Behind him a voice roared, "Run to the ends of the earth or cross the seven seas, thou shalt *never* escape my vengeance." Then came peals of titanic laughter.

Loft lashed his horse and sped away until the thunderous laughter dwindled to an echo in his ears. The night grew silent.

He rode west for several days and nights. Finally he took refuge in a small hamlet called Stadastadur, where green hills sloped down to the sea. The simple houses built of rough blocks of lava with roofs of turf were a far cry from the grand halls of the school.

Here he found the pastor kindly disposed toward him. The old man charged Loft with the upkeep of the church and grounds; in return, he promised to help Loft study Scripture.

For a long while, Loft refused to leave the blessed grounds of the church. At night he stayed indoors and would only read his Bible and pray.

But in time his fear subsided, as one day became the next and there was no sign of punishment from beyond the grave. At first Loft only dared to venture into the village on errands. Later he would sometimes stroll the outskirts of the town, or go for longer walks in the countryside.

"I have escaped the doom that Gottskalk pronounced on me," he decided. "Whatever power I gave him that night must have faded with the dawn. He cannot reach me in my new life here."

One sunny day not long after this, when the sea was calm and the sky was clear, Loft decided to row out into the cove to do some fishing. Several locals who happened to be gazing seaward later reported to the pastor that they had seen his boat bobbing on gentle waves in the windless afternoon. And they had recognized the figure of the assistant pastor fishing.

Then, to their horror, they saw a huge arm, gray as the

grave and covered with dripping seaweed, rise up out of the sea. It grabbed the boat by the stern and, in a trice, pulled it under the water.

No bit of wreckage—not so much as an oarblade—floated back to shore. Nor was Loft ever seen on earth again.

The Accursed House

(United States—Ohio)

An old farmhouse belonging to a man named Herman Deluse once stood near Gallipolis, Ohio. Though he paid scant attention to his fields or livestock, and the house was little better than a ruin, the old man never lacked for anything. He kept to himself, and discouraged his neighbors from visiting.

Many people suspected that Deluse had been a pirate. He called his place the Isle of Pines, after a notorious gathering place for buccaneers in the West Indies. On those rare occasions when the Reverend Henry Galbraith and his son William visited—the only two callers Deluse would tolerate—the man made no attempt to conceal the strange objects from distant lands and curious weapons that filled his house.

As William grew older, he asked more and more questions about the old man's source of wealth. The boy was sure that Deluse had pirate treasure hidden in the house. Though the old man never appeared to have much money at one time, he always had enough to meet his needs. And he always paid for things with old Spanish gold pieces. This convinced the people of Gallipolis—and young William in particular—that he was a former pirate. Some even suggested that he had moved so far away from the ocean because there was a price on his head.

But all William's efforts to get the old man to reveal the

source of his gold failed. Deluse remained tight-lipped, never providing any clue as to the whereabouts of his treasure—if, indeed, it existed.

When it came time for Deluse to die, he passed away alone, and was buried quietly in the nearby cemetery. Isle of Pines was locked up, while inquiries were made to determine if there were any relatives to claim the estate.

Now, it chanced that while this was going on, the Reverend Galbraith was away for a month-long visit to Cincinnati. He did not know that Herman Deluse had died. One night he returned home in the middle of a terrible storm. The snow was so deep and the road so blocked with drifts and fallen branches that he looked around for shelter.

To his relief, he saw a light. He followed it through the driving snow and recognized the Isle of Pines. As he neared the place, he noted that the light was moving about the house, brightening one darkened room after another. Whatever could old Deluse be up to? he wondered as he knocked. When no one came to the door, he rapped again even more loudly.

But still he was ignored, as the light moved from chamber to chamber. Finally, afraid of freezing to death, the reverend put his shoulder to the door and forced it open.

"Hello, Herman!" he called. "I apologize for my rude entry."

But when the old man at last appeared, carrying a candle, he paid no attention to the clergyman. Instead, he wandered about like a sleepwalker, muttering to himself, searching for something. His visitor tried to strike up a conversation, but Herman persisted in running his hands over each wall, then dropping to his knees and searching the floor.

"What have you lost?" asked the concerned Reverend Galbraith. "Can I help you search?"

Still the old man would not look at him; rather, he carried his candle to a room at the end of the passageway. In the chilly darkness, the reverend could hear him muttering over and over again. The sound made the reverend as uncomfortable as the cold. To ease his mind and body, he set about building a fire in the fireplace. Then, spreading his coat before it, he lay down, intending but a few moments' rest.

Instead, he fell into a deep sleep that lasted the better part of the night. The first light of dawn was just visible through the thinning snow when Reverend Galbraith was roused by Deluse's triumphant cry, " 'Tis here! 'Tis found!"

Pulling his coat around him, the clergyman hurried down the hall to the little room at its end. He was sure that was where the cry had come from.

But when he entered the room, he found no trace of Herman Deluse. Against the northern wall was an unlit candle stub in the curious holder that the old man had carried during his midnight search. In the dust that coated the wall, he could just make out the impression of two hands, as though someone—old Deluse, surely—had pressed his palms against the surface.

More puzzled than ever, Reverend Galbraith called out his friend's name. But though he searched from cellar to attic, he could find no trace of the man. The doors and windows were all shut tight. Nor, as he peered through the early morning dimness, could he see any footsteps in the newfallen snow.

Daunted by this mystery, Reverend Galbraith took his horse from its shelter in the tumbledown barn and continued the rest of the way home, the storm having fully abated.

.   .   .

He was welcomed by his wife and son and a good friend —a lawyer named Maren—who had come by on some bit of business that morning. But when he told his story, his wife and son merely glanced at each other, while the lawyer remarked, "Didn't you know that Deluse was dead and buried?"

The clergyman, speechless, merely shook his head.

"You must have been dreaming," said his son. But William's eyes shone with a curious light.

Reverend Galbraith insisted, "I tell you, it happened just as I said."

"If you like," said the lawyer good-naturedly, "we will go there tonight and investigate. Perhaps the ghost will appear again after dark."

"Play the fools if you want!" exclaimed William, adding, "I have business on the other side of town. I won't be back until supper."

By nine o'clock, when the lawyer came by to accompany Reverend Galbraith to Isle of Pines, William had not returned. "I'm relieved he isn't here," the clergyman confessed to Maren. "He seems to have no patience with talk of ghosts."

Together they rode out to the farm. Just as the clergyman had reported, the two men saw a light appearing first at one window, then the next. But when they drew near, the place went suddenly dark.

The front door stood open. "I know that I locked it securely when I left," said Reverend Galbraith.

Inside, all was darkness and silence. The men had brought candles, which they now lighted. In the thick dust on the floor they saw the marks of the clergyman's stay and his footprints. A second set of footprints led purposefully from the front door down the hall to the little room at its end. The door, which had been open that morning, was now shut. Flickering candlelight shone beneath it.

"Someone else has been here since you left," said the lawyer. "And I believe he is still here."

Suddenly from behind the door came a scream, then the sound of a heavy body hitting the floor, then silence.

Trembling, the two men hurried down the passage. Inside the little room they found the northern wall broken open. From the hollow space behind it several pouches had spilled their golden contents, while just below, William Galbraith lay sprawled on the floor, covered with antique Spanish coins.

With a cry, his father stooped to pick him up, then staggered back in horror, for the young man was cold and dead.

A postmortem examination revealed no cause of death, and a jury issued a verdict of death due to a "visitation of God." But Reverend Galbraith remained convinced to the end of his days that his son had been frightened to death by something quite *un*godly in that accursed farmhouse.

Escape up the Tree

(Nigeria)

There was a young man, a hunter, who had some power with charms and magic. Each day, when he set out into the forest, he would place a bowl of water in the sun. Then he would tell his mother, "If this water turns the color of blood, you will know I am in danger. Then you must unchain my three dogs and send them to rescue me."

The old woman always promised that she would do as he asked.

Now it happened that, one day while he was hunting, the young man came to a nearby village. There he found a crowd of people watching as all the unmarried young men tried to toss *ege*, tree seeds, into a hollow calabash shell. Behind the gourd knelt the most beautiful woman the hunter had ever seen.

When the young man asked what was going on, he was told that the woman had promised to marry whichever man could toss the most *ege* into the calabash.

Thinking to try his luck, the hunter took his place at the proper distance from the gourd. The woman glanced up at him and smiled. Now he was more determined than ever to win the contest. Carefully he tossed the seeds one after another into the calabash. Every seed hit its mark, a feat no one else was able to match.

At last the headman of the village declared that the

hunter had won the contest and earned the woman's hand.

She came to him shyly, but when he asked where she lived, she only said, "A great distance from here."

"Then I will take you with me to my home," the man said, "where my mother will welcome you like a daughter."

Now, despite the hunter's skills with magic, he did not realize that the young woman was really a she-devil. She had come to town seeking to lure away a man so that she could satisfy her hunger for human flesh.

After they had walked for a time, the young woman said, "Let us stop in this clearing and rest awhile. I have grown very tired."

Indeed, the young man was feeling weary himself, so he was quite willing to sit down with his back to a tree. Across from him, his bride-to-be sat watching him, smiling and licking her lips.

His eyes closed. He slept. Then an insect stung him on the shoulder, waking him. The woman across from him was no longer a woman. She was changing into a big mass of red eyes and sharp teeth.

Instantly the young man jumped up and climbed into the lower branches of the tree, just as the horror rolled across the clearing toward him. Dozens of sets of teeth snapped at his heels as he scrambled higher and higher.

Now, the she-demon could not climb the tree, but she set to work chewing the trunk, determined to topple it. The hunter recited one of the magical chants he knew, and ordered the tree to grow higher while the trunk grew thicker.

At this, the monster roared in anger. "Whatever power you have," the many mouths said together, "it will not be enough to escape me. You are going to die. I will pick your bones clean and then grind them to dust!"

So saying, the she-devil redoubled her efforts to topple the tree. Again and again the hunter used his chant, but each time he found his magic had grown weaker. The tree would grow only a tiny bit higher; the trunk would thicken only a little more.

"Why have my dogs not come to rescue me?" he wondered.

Now, his mother had taken some clothes to the stream to wash them, so she had not seen the water in the bowl turn blood red. The dogs, sensing something was amiss, were howling and trying to burst their chains. Finally the old woman at the riverbank heard them barking. Gathering up her washing, she ran to the hut.

The moment she saw the blood-red water bubbling in the pot, she gave a frightened cry. Then she unchained her son's three dogs. Instantly they raced into the woods. They reached the clearing just as the mass of teeth, busy at the base of the tree, had bitten almost all the way through the trunk.

The three huge hounds attacked the monstrous thing from all sides. As they worried it, and chased it away from the tree, the hunter slipped down and recovered his spear, which he had left lying on the ground. The dogs had already badly wounded the demon, so the hunter was able to kill it with a single thrust of his spear.

The rolling eyes grew dark; the snapping teeth were stilled; the thing shuddered and died.

Then the hunter returned home with his three dogs. There his mother, overjoyed to see him safe, prepared a great meal, to which she invited all their friends. And the hunter's three faithful dogs ate as well as any of the guests.

The Headrest

(Papua New Guinea)

In the old days, it happened that Inay, a man from the hills, came to a certain village, leading his little son by the hand. He spent the day trading with the villagers and talking with them. His boy, Mimau, sat beside him, silent and smiling shyly. People remarked what a well-behaved child he was—a blessing to his father and mother. The women kindly gave father and son taro, bananas, plantains, and sugarcane to eat.

When darkness fell, the stranger went into the *potuma*, the common house, where the men slept, to spend the night. He took his son with him. But in the *potuma* was Kakak, a man of the village who was short-tempered and violent. When he saw the hill man's child about to fall asleep beside his father, Kakak raised a great cry. While two of Kakak's friends held the hill man in check, the angry villager shook Mimau. "What are you doing here, boy?" he cried. "Don't you know that this is a house for men? Go away at once!" Then Kakak beat the little child and shoved him out of the door into the dirt beyond. The boy lay still; his spirit had fled his body.

Inay also was expelled from the *potuma*. When he saw the lifeless form of his son, he gave a cry that echoed from the distant hills. Then wordlessly, he gathered the body of his little Mimau in his arms and walked away into the night. At this Kakak boasted, "That is how I will deal with all strangers who do not respect our customs." Then, contented, he lay down to sleep.

Only a few days after this it happened that all the people of the village were fishing at the river, so no one noticed Inay creep into the empty *potuma*. When the hill man entered, he carried something in his hands; but when he left, his hands were empty. Still unseen, Inay hurried back to the hills.

At evening, the men of the village returned. After they had eaten, they went into the *potuma* and made ready to sleep, for they were weary after a day spent fishing. In the center of the sleeping place, Kakak saw a headrest carved of wood. Instantly, he claimed it for his own, saying, "This is my pillow. If any of you wish it, you must take it from me in a wrestling match—if you dare."

But the other men, knowing his fierceness and strength, refused to wrestle with him. They just shrugged and let him be. Then Kakak lay down, rested his neck on the carved wooden headrest, and was soon asleep.

In the morning, the men awoke, stretched, and one by one came out of the *potuma* into the village. But Kakak was not among them. It surprised the others that he was still sleeping, for he was usually the first to arise. After a time, one man went in and tried to rouse the fierce man. But when he looked closely, he saw that Kakak was dead. Then he made a great outcry, calling to the other men. When they saw the body, the men were very much afraid. "How could he have died so quickly and quietly?" they asked each other. "Surely he was bewitched."

Kakak was buried, and his name was no longer spoken aloud, as was the custom when someone died. But the man who had first tried to wake him took the headrest for himself. It chanced that he was one of the two who had held back the hill man while Kakak beat his child. That night he lay down to sleep. And in the morning he also was found dead.

"What evil comes into the *potuma* at night that kills men so swiftly?" the villagers wondered fearfully. "Let us watch all through the night to see what shape our enemy takes."

So the men sat up all through the night, but they saw nothing. In the morning they went wearily about their business, unsure whether the evil had truly gone away, or was merely waiting to strike again when they might be less watchful.

In the warmth of the afternoon, one man crept back to the *potuma* to sleep, while all his fellows were fishing. As it happened, this was the second of the two men who had held the hill man while his child was beaten. Seeing the headrest in a corner, he placed it under his neck, sighed contentedly, and was soon fast asleep.

Now his fellows, noticing that he was gone from the riverbank, sent a boy to fetch him. The child had just reached the entrance of the *potuma* when he saw the headrest slide out from under the sleeping man, fly into the air, then fall with great force on the sleeper's head. The man lay dead upon the ground, with the headrest beside him, before the child could so much as cry out a warning.

Fearful that the thing might fall on his own head, the boy ran back to the river, shouting to tell everyone what he had seen.

For a long time the men remained outside the common house, staring at the slain man's body and the headrest beside it. After much discussion, they gathered as much wood as possible and built a great fire in the open space outside the *potuma*. Then the strongest and bravest man went inside and picked up the headrest. To the touch, it seemed nothing more than ordinary wood. But when he neared the bonfire, the headrest began to twist about in his grip, as though it would break free.

With a cry partly of fear and partly of disgust, the man cast the headrest into the hottest part of the flames. Instantly, the wood caught fire. Then, as the villagers watched aghast, it writhed and crawled about the pyre as if it were truly alive. All the while it groaned, "A-ge-ge-ge-ge-ge!" and screamed, "A-ke-ke-ke-ke-ke!" until it was burned to ashes.

Then, from the heart of the dying fire arose a whirlwind. It carried the ashes of the headrest high into the air. There other winds caught them and carried them across the river and over the trees toward the distant hills and a village high in the mountains. They would be a sign to Inay, watching silently from the door of his hut, that vengeance had been exacted for the violence done to his little son.

The Thing in the Woods

(United States—Louisiana)

Once, in the Louisiana backwoods, there was a Cajun woman, Odette, who wanted nothing more than to have a child. But God had not granted her and her husband that gift. Sometimes she would be going about her housework when she would pause and gaze into the yard, imagining a child playing there. Her husband, Alcide, would often say, "I wish I had a son, me. That boy, when he grow up he would be best hunter in whole bayou country and Unite' States, him!"

Poor Odette spent most of her days in church, praying to the Virgin Mary. "Please let me have a *bebe* for Alcide," she would plead. "I promise I would love that child so."

But no child was sent to them.

Now, there was a stretch of woods haunted by the evil one, the devil himself. People were safe as long as they stayed on the path that ran through the forest, but they risked their lives and very souls if they strayed into the trees on either side.

When Odette was a little girl, her mother had often warned her, as she set out to school, "You be careful, Odette! You keep your feets on the road, yes. Don't you go wandering off after a flower or nothing. You walk straight to the schoolhouse and don't pay no mind to nothing else!"

But now, one spring day, as Odette was walking to church along that very road, she spied a beautiful flower growing right beside the path. It had long white petals surrounding a center as red as the finest ruby. So perfect was it that it might have been fashioned by an artist instead of growing wild. A little ways beyond it, she saw another such blossom and another.

"I will take these to church and give them to the Virgin Mary," she said. "Maybe then she will give me a *bebe*, yes?"

So she began to gather a bouquet, and didn't notice that each flower she picked led her deeper into the woods.

Suddenly she heard a sound like a child crying. Looking around anxiously, she spotted something blue under a tree. It was a bundle wrapped in blankets, from which came the child's cries. Instantly Odette dropped her flowers and ran toward it.

Swaddled in the sky-blue cloth was a handsome little baby boy, with skin as white as milk. As she reached down and gently lifted the infant in her arms, he laughed and gurgled in a way that went straight to her heart.

"Has your careless mother left you all alone here?" she asked the child. But the *bebe* only laughed and cooed even louder. Then Odette said to herself, "Maybe the Virgin has answered my prayers by sending me to find this child. I will take him home, yes. He will be a son for Alcide."

With the child gathered in her arms, the young woman hurried out of the woods. But as she neared the road, she remembered she had not thanked the Virgin for giving her this son. She carefully spread out her shawl in the shade of a tree. Upon this she gently set her blue-wrapped bundle. Then she knelt to pray.

But as soon as she had uttered the first words of her prayer, the infant began to yell and shriek. At first she tried to pray in spite of his cries. But he screamed louder and louder, almost as if her prayers were causing him pain.

At last Odette whispered to the Virgin that she would say her prayer of thanksgiving when she got home. "Let me get this *bebe* some milk and put him to bed. Then I'll pray some more, me," she promised.

So she started to pick the little one up. She raised the corner of the blanket that covered his face to speak a soothing word to the squirming baby. But when she did, her heart turned to ice.

No perfect infant with milk-white skin was in her arms. Instead she was holding something that was all black and shiny and ugly—like some beetle. And even as she watched, the thing began to grow, getting bigger and bigger by the minute. Poor Odette was so frightened that she nearly died on the spot.

She dropped the writhing bundle on the ground. To her horror she found she couldn't move: Her legs felt like they were rooted to the spot. Not knowing what else to do, she made the sign of the cross in the air over the tangled blanket, from which two shiny black claws had emerged.

To her everlasting relief, she found that she had done the right thing. The evil one hates the mark of the cross. The creature that was still half hidden gave a yell like forty devils. Then Odette saw something that looked partly like a giant beetle, and partly like a little hunched-up man with shiny insect skin, run off into the woods.

As soon as its cries had died away, Odette found that she could move again.

Still shaking, she hastened directly to the church, where she thanked God and the Virgin for her escape.

The very next day, Alcide and Odette moved far away to Bayou Barataria. There they made a new life for them-

selves, and in time they were blessed with a family of five sons and four daughters. Odette was careful to see that each child said his or her prayers day and night, went to church faithfully, and never went picking flowers in the woods.

King of the Cats

(British Isles—England)

On a chilly winter's evening, a gravedigger's wife sat by the fireside, waiting for her husband to come home. Across from her sat her big black cat, Old Tom, who was half asleep, like his mistress.

"Wherever can the man be?" the woman asked.

"Meow," said Old Tom, stretching his legs.

So they waited and waited.

Suddenly both jumped to hear footsteps pounding up the path. A minute later, the gravedigger, all out of breath, came rushing into the room.

"Who's Tom Tildrum?" he shouted in such a wild way that both his wife and his cat stared at him in surprise.

"Why, what's the matter?" asked his wife. "And why do you want to know who Tom Tildrum is?"

The gravedigger caught his breath and pulled a chair up to the fire. "What an adventure I've had! There I was, digging away at old Mr. Fordyce's grave. Hard work it was, so I paused for a rest, sitting in the hole itself, where the wind couldn't reach me. Then I suppose I dropped off to sleep. How long I remained so, I can't say. But I woke up when I heard a cat's *meow*."

"Meow," said Old Tom in answer.

"Yes, just like that! So I peeped over the edge of the grave, and what do you think I saw?"

"Now, how could I know that?" his wife said. "Get on with the telling."

"Indeed, I saw nine black cats that looked for all the world like our own Tom here," said her husband. "Each had a white spot on its chest, just like him. And what do you think they were carrying?" he asked his wife.

"You might as well ask Old Tom as ask me," said his wife, who was growing impatient, "since we were both of us sitting by the fire."

"Well, those cats were walking upright, and eight of them were carrying a little coffin on their shoulders. It was covered with a black velvet cloth, and the cloth was all bordered in little gold crowns. The ninth cat—bigger than the others—walked in front. At every third step, he would call out, 'Meow!' Then the others would all answer together, 'Meow!' "

"Meow!" wailed Old Tom again.

"Yes, just like that!" exclaimed the gravedigger. "And as they came nearer and nearer to me, I could see them even more clearly, because their eyes seemed to shine with a strange green light. Well, they all came toward me, and the leader looked for all the world like—but look at our Tom!" the man said, pointing a finger at the cat on the hearth. "See how he's staring at me! You'd think he understood every word I was saying."

"Go on, go on," said his wife. "Never mind Old Tom."

"Well, as I was saying," the gravedigger continued, "those cats came slowly toward me, marching as solemnly as proper mourners, and every third step crying out, 'Meow!' in answer to the leader's own 'Meow!' "

"Meow!" bawled Old Tom again.

"Yes, just like that," the man said with a nod. "On they came, until they stood alongside Mr. Fordyce's grave. There they stood still and stared right at me. It made me feel odd, that it did! Those nine pair of glowing green eyes peering at me." Then the man looked at his own cat and

said, "But look at Old Tom. He's staring at me just the way they did. And—bless me!—but there seems to be more green in his eyes than I've ever seen before."

"Go on, go on," said his wife, "finish the story and never mind Old Tom!"

"Where was I?" said the man. "Oh, yes, I recall now. Those nine big cats just stood still, looking at me. Then the one that wasn't carrying the coffin came forward, stood on the edge of the grave gazing down at me, and said—"

"Are you saying that the cat *spoke* to you?" his wife asked, shaking her head in disbelief.

Now it was her husband's turn to grow impatient. "*Yes,* I swear to you, he said to me, in a squeaky voice, 'Tell Tom Tildrum that Tim Toldrum is dead.' I was so unnerved, I ran from the churchyard that very minute. And that's why, when I first came in here, I asked you if you know who Tom Tildrum is. How can I tell Tom Tildrum that Tim Toldrum is dead, if I don't for the life of me know who Tom Tildrum is?"

But his wife suddenly shouted, "Look at Old Tom! *Look at Old Tom!*"

Then the both of them gaped, for Old Tom seemed to grow to twice his normal size, while his eyes blazed with a terrible green light. He shrieked out, "What? Old Tim dead? Then *I'm* King of the Cats!"

With a howl of triumph he rushed up the chimney and was nevermore seen by the gravedigger or his wife.

The Dead Mother

(Russia)

Long, long ago, in the days when the czars ruled Russia, a husband and wife lived in a small village. Though they were poor, and their life from day to day was always hard, they remained happy and loving. The mere sight of Ivan and Anya walking hand-in-hand gave pleasure to their neighbors; their shared joy lightened the labors of farmhand and housewife alike.

When the couple found out that they were to have a child, they were delighted. This was the miracle they had been praying for for years. Now their dearest dream would be fulfilled.

But a dark cloud cast its shadow over their happiness. Shortly after Anya bore a son, she died with the infant resting in her arms. To the last, the poor woman's eyes were fixed on the sweet, tiny face of her sleeping child. The sadness and longing in her eyes shattered the already breaking heart of her husband. A moment later, she sighed her last. Then poor Ivan dropped to his knees beside the bed, holding his wife's cold hand, and moaned and wept until his cries woke the child.

Gently he gathered his son into his arms. How was he to bring up his motherless child alone? he wondered. He determined to do the best that he could. So he hired an old woman named Tatiana to look after the baby while he worked in the fields.

But a strange thing happened. All day long the infant would cry endlessly, refusing all food, refusing to be comforted. Yet, during the deepest hours of the night, he remained so quiet that neither Ivan nor old Tatiana sleeping beside the child's cradle was ever disturbed. One might have thought the baby wasn't there at all.

The old woman grew increasingly worried about why a child so fretful by day should remain strangely silent throughout the night. It seemed to her unnatural. Finally, determined to get to the bottom of the mystery, she decided to stay awake and watch until dawn.

The next night, having settled the baby (who had fussed the whole day) as best she could in his cradle, Tatiana sat on the bench near the hearth. By the fire's glow she mended one of Ivan's shirts. From the room behind the curtain she could hear the man's soft snoring.

As the hour grew late, the baby stopped crying. When Tatiana leaned over the cradle to see if he was asleep, she was surprised to find the baby wide-eyed, with a look on his tiny face that suggested he was watching and listening for something. When the infant first saw her, he smiled and stretched his little arms up to her. Then he seemed to recognize her, and screwed up his face as though he would burst into tears. Startled, the old woman stepped back. Instantly the child sighed, and became as quiet and watchful as before.

Puzzled, Tatiana retreated to her corner by the fireplace. She took up her mending, but kept her eyes on the cradle, hardly daring to breathe. An expectant hush had fallen on the room.

Suddenly, just at midnight, she heard someone softly open the door. Looking up, she saw the figure of a woman, shrouded in veils, tiptoe to the cradle. Tatiana tried to call out, but her voice was frozen in her throat as surely as she herself was frozen to the bench.

The stranger's veils were draped over the cradle. From beneath came the sound of the infant's contented gurgling and occasional chuckles of pleasure.

After what seemed like hours, the veiled figure abandoned the cradle and once again tiptoed to the door. When the door was opened, Tatiana could see streaks of dawn light to the east.

The moment the door shut behind the figure, the old woman was able to rise. She ran to the cradle and looked in, but the baby was sleeping peacefully. Yanking the cottage door wide, she gazed across the yard, which was lightly powdered with the first snow of winter. But she saw no trace of the mysterious woman. Not so much as a single footprint marred the smooth expanse of snow.

Uncertain whether she had really seen anything, or had merely fallen asleep beside the fireplace and dreamed it, the old woman decided to say nothing to Ivan. She would keep watch a second night to see what happened.

But the next night, the same thing happened.

When it happened the third night, she told Ivan what she had seen. Deeply troubled, he called together his kinsfolk to ask their advice on what to do.

After much discussion, they decided to stay with Ivan that same night, to see who came to visit the infant in the dead of night. As soon as the sun set, they all lay down on the floor. Ivan rested with them, with a lighted candle hidden beneath an old earthen pot beside his head. The baby, as though troubled by so many people around his cradle, seemed more restless than ever.

At midnight, the door of the cottage slowly opened, just as Tatiana had said. A silken rustling and the sounds of someone tiptoeing toward the cradle could be heard by all. At that instant, the baby ceased his crying and began to gurgle happily. But the watchers felt their limbs growing heavy and their voices catching in their throats. Only Ivan

was able to resist the weariness long enough to reach over and uncover the candle.

In the light, the spell was broken. Ivan scrambled to his feet and held out the taper toward the veiled figure. His eyes grew wide with astonishment and fear when he recognized his beloved Anya, clad in the very same clothes in which she had been buried. She was on her knees beside the cradle, clutching the child to her heart.

Ivan whispered her name as he took a step closer. But the candle suddenly blazed up. At the same instant, she set the infant down in the crib and gazed mournfully at her tiny son. Then she turned and left the room without a sound, with never a word to Ivan or any of his kinsfolk who stood around the chamber, terror-struck.

Ivan stared as the door closed gently behind Anya. Then, with a soft moan, he stooped and picked up the baby. But his moan quickly turned to cries of anguish when he realized that the child he held in his arms was dead.

Knock . . . Knock . . . Knock . . .

(United States/Canada—urban folklore)

You're wearing *that* to a costume party?" exclaimed Nicole. "That's not a *costume*."

"I'm going as a jogger," said Mark.

"You jog every day. That's only your old gray running suit!"

"So, it's authentic," Mark said. "Anyhow, I didn't have time to come up with a real costume."

"You could have rented one," Nicole pointed out.

"I'm not wasting my hard-earned college money on a giant bunny outfit," he said. "Besides, you're dressed up enough for both of us."

"I'm Queen Guinevere," she explained. "You know, she married King Arthur."

"Yeah, I saw the movie on TV," Mark said. "Um, Nic. Just to put you on yellow alert, my car's been giving me a little trouble."

Nicole sighed. "Will it get us there?"

"Ninety-eight percent certainty."

"And back?" she wondered, then added quickly, "Don't give me the odds: Just get us there. We'll work the rest out later."

"You got it!" Mark said, offering her his arm. "Queen Guinevere, your Toyota awaits."

"Lancelot you're not," she said, laughing. "But you do look pretty good—even in a grungy jogging suit."

. . .

However, Nicole's high spirits soon evaporated. Mark's car managed nearly to stall out at every stop sign or intersection.

"Are you sure we'll get to the country club?" she asked anxiously.

"Yeah, I'm sure," Mark snapped as the engine sputtered and the car shuddered.

Nicole held her breath, but the problem seemed to correct itself. It wasn't just the car that made her jittery; a heavy fog had settled over the lonely, twisting country road.

"Relax, put on some music," Mark suggested, adding quickly, "—um, on the radio. The cassette player is broken."

Nicole almost said something about what bad shape everything was in, but she decided not to risk an argument. As the hills grew higher, the music stations faded into static. All she could get was a news station.

"Great," she said, making a face. Then she paused, listening intently, as the radio announced:

". . . warning everyone in the Norris Valley area that convicted killer Owen Helms—the so-called Hangman— has escaped from the criminal asylum at Pinecrest . . ."

"That's just at the other end of the valley!" cried Nicole. She was going to *insist* that Mark turn the car around, when two things happened. The radio program dissolved into crackling static, and the car bucked twice and died. Mark used what momentum was left to steer the Toyota to the side of the road. They came to a stop under a tree. Condensed fog dripped from an overhanging branch, *thunk, thunk, thunk.*

Mark turned the ignition key several times, but all the engine would do was gurgle and chuff. Soon even these noises grew weaker. The car refused to start.

Finally Nicole said, "Give it a rest; you're just draining the battery."

Mark slammed his fist against the steering wheel. Then he climbed out, lifted the hood, and fiddled with the engine.

"Try it now!" he'd call every few minutes. But when Nicole turned the key, all she got were clicks. In between, she tried to get some more news on the escaped killer. But the radio just gave off creepy sounds like whispers, so she snapped it off.

"I'm going to have to go and get help. Lucky I wore my jog togs and Nikes after all. I think we're just a few miles from the country club. I'll call a tow truck from there, then have someone bring me back here. I shouldn't be gone more than a half hour or so."

"No way am I staying out here by myself," said Nicole. "Not with the Happy Hangman on the loose."

"Be reasonable, Nic! How are you gonna jog in that costume of yours? And I'm not about to go for a stroll through this freezing fog."

"No, Mark, *please!*"

"If you're really worried, crouch down on the floor in back under the old blanket. If anyone comes along, they'll think the car is empty. But no one will bother you, I promise."

"You also promised to get us to the party," she said. But she was more scared than angry. "Oh, all right—but I *swear* I'm not coming out from under that blanket until I'm sure it's you."

"I'm gonna leave you the keys for safekeeping. When I get back, I'll knock three times, like this." He went *knock . . . knock . . . knock . . .* on the roof of the car, just above the door on the driver's side. "Don't come out until you hear that signal."

"I won't," she said, "believe me."

He kissed her good-bye, watched while she locked and tested both doors, then waved as he jogged away into the fog. The minute he was out of sight, she climbed into the backseat, bunched up in the narrow space, and arranged the musty old blanket over herself.

How long she remained there Nicole wasn't sure. When her legs began to cramp, she brought her watch up to her face without disturbing the blanket and read the illuminated dial. Less than half an hour had passed, but it felt more like years.

Suddenly she heard a *knock* on the roof of the car.

"Mark," she whispered. She was about to throw off the blanket, when she remembered he'd promised to knock *three* times. She had a sudden, sickening feeling that someone else was outside—maybe trying to find a way into the locked car.

"Please, please, knock again," she whispered. "Make it be Mark!"

Knock.

"Once more—please; just once more."

Knock.

She almost laughed out loud with relief . . .

Knock.

Her blood turned to ice water.

Knock . . . knock . . . knock . . .

She froze, hardly daring to breathe, as the knocks continued on and on, spaced just about the same. Each one was like a fist in her stomach.

At first she was sure that the Hangman was trying to get in. Then she imagined that he was so wacko that he was just beating on the car like a child pounding endlessly on a toy drum. Finally she wondered if he *knew* she was inside, and was tormenting her until he smashed a window.

Knock . . . knock . . . knock . . .

"Please, someone, come help me!" she prayed.

Knock . . . knock . . .

Then she heard the sound of heavy boots crunching on the gravel. Voices. And a radio, with a dispatcher's voice giving instructions that she couldn't make out.

Knock.

Then, mercifully, it stopped. Mark must have come. Or the tow truck. Nicole sat up and looked out the window—and screamed!

Two men were staring in at her. After a terrifying, confused moment, she realized that they were police. Behind them she saw the spinning blue and red lights on top of their police car.

"It's okay, young lady," the first officer said. "You can come out now."

Her shaking hand found the lock release. She climbed unsteadily out.

"Where's Mark?" she asked, looking around. "Didn't he come with you?"

"Come to the patrol car," said the second officer. "*Don't look back*—just keep your eyes on the patrol car."

"Why can't I look?" Nicole asked. She turned suddenly and saw Mark's body, still in the gray jogging outfit, hanging from the tree limb above the car.

"Hey!" yelled the officer. "You don't want to see this, miss!" As he reached out to grab her the body started swinging. Nicole watched in horror as one Nike-clad foot began to beat against the roof of the car:

Knock . . . knock . . . knock . . .

Twice Surprised

(Japan)

Late one winter night, a schoolteacher was walking along a road that ran beside a rice field. To his surprise, he discovered a lovely young woman seated on a large, white stone at the edge of the field. Her face was hidden from him as she read, by moonlight, a book spread open on her lap.

Surprised to find anyone else on the lonely road so late, the man greeted her politely. She nodded, but did not look up from her book.

"What text are you studying so carefully?" he asked.

Still, she did not answer him or look up.

Finally the teacher said lightly, "Is it wise for you to be alone out here so late at night? This is the hour when ghosts are prowling about, you know. Perhaps I am a ghost myself."

She did not respond to his little joke, but she looked up at him. The top half of her face was a mass of ghastly, glittering eyes all different sizes and colors. The lower half of her face split wide open from side to side, revealing a serpent's jaws with bared fangs. From deep within her throat came a warning growl.

One look at her horrible face, and the teacher fled in terror, his coat thrown over his head for fear he might see that ghastly face again.

The unfortunate man was gasping for breath and still trembling when he reached his home. Though the house

71

was quite warm, he felt as cold as if he were lost in the heart of a blizzard.

His wife, without looking up from the letter she was writing, asked him, "Why are you so out of breath and distressed?"

"I saw something horrible on my way home," her husband answered. "It must have been a ghost or a demon."

"What did it look like?" she asked.

"It appeared, in the moonlight, to be a beautiful young woman," he said.

"If she was beautiful," his wife asked, her inkbrush gracefully shaping characters on the page in front of her, "why were you frightened?"

"When she looked up at me, her face was horrible! *Horrible!*" said the man, beginning to shake again.

"What did it look like?" his wife asked.

"I cannot describe it," the poor man said, "it was so terrible. One cannot capture in words how frightful that face was."

"But what did it look like?" his wife persisted.

"I cannot tell you what it looked like," the teacher answered helplessly.

"Was it this kind of face?" his wife asked. So saying, she turned away from her letter, toward her husband. Before him was the horrible face he had seen in the moonlight. But now it seemed to grow until it filled the room with dreadful eyes and teeth.

Scared out of his wits, the man gave a cry of terror, then sank senseless to the floor.

When he awoke the next morning, the sun was shining brightly on him as he lay facedown beside a large white stone at the edge of the road.

Appointment in Samarra

(Persia)

Among those who lived in Persia, many once believed Death took the form of a tall woman, hooded in black. In this guise she could sometimes be seen wandering the bazaars of great cities. At first glance, she seemed to be only another shopper. But when she was recognized, she was shunned by mortals, who fled in fear of her gaze or touch.

One afternoon, Rakush, the servant of the wealthiest merchant in Baghdad, went early to market to purchase foods for a banquet his master planned for the evening. But as he haggled with a seller over the price of pomegranates, he glanced up and was horrified to see the tall, reedy figure of Death, swathed in black, staring at him from a neighboring stall. When their eyes met, Death pointed her finger at him and started to speak.

Dropping his basket of pomegranates and clapping his hands to his ears to avoid hearing the voice of Death, Rakush fled the market. Behind him, the stallkeeper scrambled to pick up the spilled fruit, and called down ruin upon Rakush's head and household. The vendor did not notice the tall, hooded figure who gazed thoughtfully after the fleeing man.

Rakush did not stop running until he reached his master's house. There, to the astonishment of the merchant, Rakush flung himself at his master's feet.

"Forgive me, Master," pleaded Rakush. "This very morning I saw Death in the marketplace. She stared right at me and made a threatening gesture with her hand."

Overcome with horror at the memory, the man shuddered and buried his pale face in his shaking hands.

When he could speak again, he kissed the merchant's slippers. "Oh, Master, I beg you: loan me your fastest horse so that I may flee to far Samarra, where my cousin lives. There I may escape the clutches of Death."

"Of course," said the merchant, who was a kind-hearted man. "Take the horse and go at once. Allah bring you safely to Samarra."

Rakush departed hastily, lashing his borrowed horse to breakneck speed. Meanwhile the merchant went to the bazaar, to see whether Death would appear and to pray her not to be angry that his servant had escaped his fate.

Shortly after entering the marketplace, the merchant spotted Death. Hooded in black, she idled among the stands, examining the wares on display. From time to time she would tap a man or woman on the shoulder, as if to ask the quality of the goods. But each person touched would stifle a cry of fear and hurry away.

Nevertheless, the merchant was a righteous man who had confidence in the mercy of Allah—so much so that Death herself did not daunt him. So he beckoned the tall, black-cowled figure to him; and she came willingly enough.

"I am curious as to why you threatened my servant," he said.

"I never threatened him," answered Death with just the hint of a smile. "I simply made a gesture of surprise at seeing him here in Baghdad. You see, I have an appointment with him tonight in Samarra."

And with a chuckle, she disappeared.

Deer Woman

(United States—Ponca tribe)

Long ago, the Ponca people lived in what is now Nebraska. They dwelt in mat houses, cooked their meat in clay pots, and carved their weapons from stone and wood. But during a time of peace and plenty, the tribe was troubled by a fearful spirit called the Deer Woman.

One night, there was a big dance to celebrate a successful buffalo hunt. The old men built a big fire; and the young women danced around it, stepping sidewise in a ring. The young men danced apart, leaping and prancing in the space between the bonfire and the circling women.

One young man, Gray Hawk, paused and looked up. There, between two young women he knew, holding their hands, was a stranger—the most beautiful woman he had ever seen. Her hair flowed like a black waterfall over her white buckskin dress. Though it was impolite, he stared into her enchanting, deep, black eyes. While everyone around him danced and laughed and sang, he could only gaze into the lovely face of the young woman.

At last the woman stretched out her hand and drew him aside. Her eyes never left his; he was captured, and the thought pleased him. As the moon sank to its lowest point, she led him away into the shadows beyond the firelit circle of dancers.

Now, Gray Hawk had a younger brother, Many Arrows, who watched what was happening. He felt uneasy, wondering who this woman was who had charmed his elder brother. When Gray Hawk left with the young woman, Many Arrows hesitated, then decided to follow.

To his horror he found Gray Hawk trampled to death, his body slashed and scarred by knife-edged hooves. The tracks of a huge deer were clearly imprinted in the earth. Many Arrows saw no moccasin prints except his brother's. What had become of the young woman?

Many Arrows carried his brother's broken body back to the Ponca camp, raising a great cry.

There the oldest woman in the village told Many Arrows that his brother had been lured away and destroyed by Deer Woman. She told the grieving young man there was nothing he could do to prevent the creature's coming and going among them. There was a great power in the demon woman. Anyone who gazed into her eyes saw just her loveliness and would be bewitched. Only if one could keep his eyes cast down would he see that her feet were a deer's hooves, which no moccasins would fit.

But Many Arrows vowed revenge. Before the next gathering, a seven-foot wall of brush and logs was built around the dance ring at his request. When the dancing began and all the people of the village were inside the circle, some men sealed the entrance with a gate of branches.

The fire was lit; the women began dancing around the inside of the ring's wall. Many Arrows had made the other men of the village promise not to look up at the women's faces, but to keep their eyes on the dancers' feet so that they could watch for the telltale hooves and not fall under Deer Woman's spell.

But as the dance went on, the young men could not

resist looking at the pretty women dancing around them. Soon only Many Arrows refused to look up. So it was that he saw, in the shuffling line of moccasins, the sudden appearance of a pair of huge deer hooves.

With a cry, Many Arrows threw himself at Deer Woman and grabbed for her. What had seemed to be a lovely woman suddenly became a huge deer wearing the shreds of a woman's skirt. The young man tried to wrestle the creature to the ground, but she slashed at him with her knife-sharp hooves. Then, with an unearthly cry, the demoness leapt over the seven-foot wall.

By the time the young man and his fellows wrenched open the gate and followed with drawn bows, the ghostly creature was bounding away across the moonlit grassland, beyond the reach of any arrow. Though they tried tracking the creature in the morning, the trail soon vanished.

After this, the dancers were always on the watch for Deer Woman, but she never returned. From time to time, though, stories reached the Ponca people about a young man in some other village who had lost his life to the fearsome spirit.

The Maggot

(British Isles—England)

In Yorkshire, years ago, a loathsome creature haunted the churchyard of a little village.

The first person to see it was the postman, Ian Thwaite. One moonlit night, he passed the graveyard on his way home. Through the gate he saw a large blob of glowing ooze rise from the grave of a recently dead villager. A horrible, wriggling mix of maggot and glowworm, it grew bigger and bigger as it emerged. The thing's eyes gave off a blaze of pure evil—yet they struck Ian as disturbingly human, too.

The thing twisted snakelike around the tombstones, finally pushing out through the gate pickets, while Ian watched from behind a nearby bush.

Horrified yet fascinated, he followed the huge maggot at a safe distance. The road was empty as the ghastly apparition moved along like a caterpillar, leaving a trail of gleaming slime. This lingered briefly, then faded without a trace. Ian was careful not to step on any part of the road touched by the sickening stuff.

The monstrosity's destination proved to be the nearby home of the vicar. As Ian watched, shivering from revulsion as much as from the night air, the thing oozed across the threshold of the vicar's cottage. Then the glowing worm began to push beneath the front door. In a trice, it vanished inside.

The postman felt dizzy, overwrought by what he had seen. He sat down suddenly. The starry sky spun overhead. He blacked out for a moment.

When he came to, the vicar's cottage was quiet. Surely if the postman had seen what he thought he had seen, the house would have been in an uproar. Deciding that he had had an awful waking dream, Ian hurried home to his bed. But his sleep was plagued with nightmares of being pursued by wormy things burning bright as coals.

At dinner the next day, he and his wife, Edna, were joined by a friend, William West. The others asked Ian why he seemed so nervous and preoccupied. When he told them his experience, he expected them to laugh. But they believed he might have witnessed some supernatural event; both suggested that they all go to the churchyard and watch, and see if the apparition would appear again.

They waited until dark. Then, leaving Ian and Edna's five-year-old son in the care of the housekeeper, the three adults took up watch outside the churchyard. Though he felt better having the others with him, Ian was not eager to face his nightmare again.

Just as before, the glowing maggot extruded itself from the new grave, retraced its course to the vicar's cottage, and squeezed through the gap under the door.

This time, however, Edna did not hesitate to rap loudly on the door. The vicar himself, looking tired and cross, opened the door. When he found it was not a parishioner needing his services, but a group of excited neighbors with a story of giant, glowing worms, he grew quite annoyed. He assured the three that he had walked the length of the house to answer the door, and that nothing was amiss. He obviously thought they had all gone mad.

When he closed the door, the sound was loud and emphatic.

Talking softly, husband and wife returned home, while William went his own way.

Ian and Edna were having tea the next day when William charged up the path and pounded on the door. As soon as they let him in, he breathlessly told them that the vicar and his family had been taken ill the night before, and all had died by noon. The doctor said the deaths were from food poisoning, probably from some tainted fish they had eaten.

"I suspect a very different cause," said Ian grimly.

His wife and friend nodded in agreement.

More determined than ever to get to the bottom of the haunting, the three again took up watch at the churchyard that night.

Once more, the disgusting, glowing maggot wriggled up from the earth and slithered out of the cemetery. They followed the trail of fading slime to the house of the blacksmith. But their attempt to warn the man was turned away with laughter and the accusation that they were all "daft." This time, one visit from the maggot was enough. The blacksmith became ill in the morning and was dead before day's end. Again the doctor called it food poisoning, and he warned people to be more careful preparing meals.

Increasingly worried, Ian and his companions stood guard a third night. Sure enough, the horror arose from the grave. This time they realized too late that it was headed for Ian and Edna's house! They broke into a run as the thing reached their porch and flowed under the door.

The three burst into the house. Frantically they

searched every room, every cupboard, every chest, but not a trace of the thing could they find. All the while, the housekeeper tried to hush their son, who was upset by the commotion.

Ian and William decided to keep watch through the night. Edna took the child into her bed and kept her own uneasy watch.

Despite their efforts, the boy was stricken with a fever in the morning. The doctor came at once, but nothing he did helped. The child grew worse. When the doctor spoke vaguely of food poisoning, the others pointed out that they had eaten the same food, and they were fine. The priest was then summoned, in the hope that prayer might achieve what medicine could not.

But there was no remedy. The child died at noon.

For Ian and Edna and William, grief was mixed with a desire for revenge. That night, they marched back to the churchyard, carrying a hooded lantern and shovels. There they dug into the grave that housed the maggot.

The grave belonged to Malcolm Sharpe, a wretched man who had made life miserable for his neighbors— often threatening one or another with harm for some imagined offense. He had taken a particular dislike to the vicar and the blacksmith.

When they unearthed the coffin, Ian and William pried up the lid while Edna held the lantern. Inside, they found the body cold but uncorrupted. Sharpe's open eyes burned with a look of intense evil. From between the corpse's grinning lips a liquid brightness began to seep. In terror, Ian slammed the lid down.

The men scrambled out of the hole and doused the coffin with kerosene. When it had burned to cinders, Edna sprinkled it with holy water she had taken from the church. Then they filled in the grave and kept uneventful watch until dawn.

The hideous specter was never seen after this. Ian and Edna mourned their son, and always regretted that their efforts to stop the evil had brought such sorrow. But they took comfort in knowing that they had kept the maggot from harming any other villager.

Witch Woman

(United States—African American traditional)

Late one night, a traveler down South lost his way in a dreary swamp. He was exhausted and desperate for shelter, and faint with hunger, when he spotted a lonely cabin. Encouraged by the light in the cabin's single window, he rapped at the door.

An old woman answered. Though her skin was wrinkled, it had the sheen of hand-rubbed leather. Her eyes were soft, and shone in the light of the candle she held. For all her years, she moved with the easy grace of a cat.

Hat in hand, the man politely said, "If I can just get me a hunk of corn pone and a slice of bacon, and maybe a place to bed down, I'd be willing to pay anything."

"Anything?" asked the woman with a curious smile.

"Truth, ma'am, I ain't got but a few pennies," said the traveler. "But you're welcome to 'em if you can spare me even a crust of bread."

Her smile grew bigger. "I don't want your coins," she said. "But I can give you better than a crust of bread. And you'll have a place to sleep. Come in. In the morning, you can do some chores for me."

The hungry man's mouth began to water when he saw a well-filled skillet cooking over the hot coals in the fireplace. The smell of frying ham made his stomach growl.

The woman sat him at a table. Then she gave him a

plate heaped with meat and greens and corn bread. It tasted so good that he ate until he felt fit to burst.

After all the food, he was ready to sleep. He reminded her that she had promised him a bed for the night.

"You can sleep in the woodshed," she answered. "But mind that you don't bother me until morning. I'm an old woman. I need my rest." At this, she smiled the biggest smile ever.

The man gratefully took the bit of blanket she gave him and made himself a bed in the woodshed. But once he had bedded down, he found he couldn't sleep. A night wind circled the shed restlessly. The cries of an owl, and chirrings and scratchings under the floorboards, disturbed him.

Across the yard, he saw the old woman's window blazing brightly. If she was still awake, he decided, he would go and talk with her. The night was spooking him that much.

To be sure that she wasn't asleep, he peeked in the window.

To his surprise he saw the woman doing a juba dance in the middle of the floor. She stopped and took a big gridiron down from the wall and raked it full of hot coals from the fireplace. Then she hauled her spinning wheel over and sat down on the gridiron. Soon her skin seemed to glow as red-hot as the coals.

Suddenly she pinched a bit of her chin's skin between her fingers, drew it threadlike to the spinning wheel, and began to spin the skin right off her body. Over and over she sang,

Spin and turn,
Burn, coal, burn,

Turn and spin,
Come off, skin.

In horror, the man watched her spin all the skin off her body. As the skin-threads pulled away, they revealed an enormous, tawny-yellow cat underneath. The creature pushed the heap of unraveled skin under the bed, saying, "Lie there, skin. I've got business to tend to. Tomorrow, when that fellow has done his chores, I'll have him for supper."

Cackling, she leapt through the window, while the man hid. Then the cat bounded into the forest as fast as a panther.

With the creature out in the swamp, the man didn't dare run off. Yet it would be worse when she returned. At first, he thought his situation was hopeless. Then he had an idea.

Slipping into the cabin, he dragged the skin from under the bed. Then he poured pepper and salt into the witch woman's skin. Finally he put the skin back under the bed. Shaking with nervousness, he went back to the woodshed.

Hours passed as he waited, trembling. At last he heard heavy paws pad toward the cabin. There was silence. He held his breath, peeking through a knothole. Suddenly terrible screams and moans erupted from inside the cabin. The witch stumbled into the yard, trying to pull off her old-woman skin.

"You did this!" she bellowed, pointing her finger at the woodshed. Still tugging at her skin, she lunged across the yard. As she did, she began to change into something that was half cat, half woman.

Thunk! She flung herself at the cabin door. *Thump! Thump!* For a minute he held the door shut. Then the creature's weight splintered the old wood. Cat's paws at the ends of human arms snatched at him, but he skedaddled backward, up the pile of sawn logs behind him. The stacked wood collapsed and rolled toward the snarling cat-woman. She stumbled and fell, just long enough for him to get out the door.

She didn't follow. He crept back—close enough to see that the salt and pepper had vexed her so that all she could think about was pulling off her old skin. She didn't notice the sun beginning to rise.

The man turned to run when the cat-shape, free of the salted skin, leapt into the yard. But the witchy thing was meant only for night. When the sunlight touched the creature's fur, it gave a terrifying yowl and fell down dead. Without another look, the traveler fled into the lightening forest.

The Berbalangs

(Philippines)

Over a century ago, Andrew Simmons, a British traveler, visited the little island of Cagayan Sulu, a lonely spot of land in the Sulu Sea between the Philippine islands and Malaysia. Simmons was intrigued by strange tales of a village at the center of the island inhabited by "Berbalangs," who only looked like humans. It was said that they were cannibals who had cats' eyes. When the hunger for human flesh drove them, they would lie down in the tall grass. Then they would fall into a trance and send their winged spirits hunting for victims, while their bodies stayed hidden in the grass.

The people of Cagayan Sulu lived in fear of their unearthly neighbors. They warned Simmons that Berbalang hunters made a moaning noise, which was loud at a distance but died away to near silence as they approached their prey. When they were very close, the sound of their wings would be heard, and their flashing eyes would dance like fireflies in the dark.

Simmons was told that a coconut pearl (a stone like an opal, sometimes found in a coconut) would keep him safe. Without one, the only defense was a *kris* (knife) that had its blade rubbed with lime juice. Simmons offered to buy a coconut pearl, but he learned that the pearl only protects the one who finds it, losing its power if given away or sold.

Determined to find the truth behind the frightening stories, Simmons vowed to visit the ghoulish tribe. At first, he could get no one to guide him. Finally one brave young man, Matali, agreed to accompany him.

They set out the next morning from the seaside village. After a difficult trek, they sighted their destination late in the afternoon. Simmons wanted to push on, but Matali refused to go closer than half a mile. "You have seen the place," he said to the Englishman. "Let us go."

"I haven't come this far to stop now," Simmons replied.

Matali shrugged, making clear he would go no farther. But the young Filipino smeared his *kris* with lime juice and handed it to his companion. Thus armed, Simmons entered the village alone. The two dozen or so huts seemed unremarkable; but, except for a few chickens and a goat, no living thing could be seen. The Englishman entered several huts but found them deserted. In one, some rice was standing in a pot, still quite hot, as if the occupants had left just before their meal.

When Simmons told Matali about the deserted village, the young man begged the older one to hurry away with him, saying that the empty huts meant the Berbalangs were hunting in their winged form. It was dangerous to be anywhere near.

The sun was setting as the two began their hasty journey home. Before they had covered half the distance, it grew dark. Not a breath of air stirred. The woods were unnaturally silent.

They had just started across a treeless valley when they heard loud moaning. Matali immediately crouched down in the long grass and signaled Simmons to hide. "The Berbalangs!" he whispered. "Pray they pass without seeing us." Though the Englishman was doubtful, Matali's fear was real enough. Simmons knelt also.

The moaning grew fainter. Matali whispered that the hunters were coming closer.

Suddenly the sound died away to a faint hum, and the sound of wings could be clearly heard. A swarm of dancing lights—like fireflies, only reddish—swept over the tall grasses. Simmons gasped as Matali gripped his arm painfully. When the lights halted and began to circle as if attracted to something in the tall grass, Simmons felt the hair on his head begin to rise.

Then the lights passed on, the noise of the wings ceased, and the moaning grew louder. "They have gone," Matali said. "We are safe for a while."

Staying in the shadows, alert for the flickering red lights, they raced for Matali's village. Once, they saw the lights of an isolated house, far from the path. To their horror they heard moaning, loud at first, but growing fainter. Above the roof swirled countless red specks, like chimney sparks.

"We must help those people," said Simmons.

"Hassan, who owns the house, has a coconut pearl to protect him," said Matali. "Hurry! This is our chance to escape."

Simmons hurried.

In the morning, Simmons chided himself for having been fool enough to let Matali's fear and the swarming fireflies scare him.

When Simmons asked about the man, Hassan, Matali confessed that he had lied about Hassan's having a coconut pearl. Hassan had arrived only recently. He was a scholar who was studying the history and culture of the island, and he laughed off stories about the Berbalangs.

"Sounds like a man after my own heart," said Simmons. "I'll pay him a visit. He's sure to have some interesting views."

When the Englishman reached Hassan's house, no one answered his knock, but the latch gave way and the door swung open. Calling Hassan's name, Simmons entered the house. The shades of split bamboo were rolled down, so the place was in deep shadow. He could make out a desk littered with books and papers.

Suddenly he backed away with a gasp.

Huddled on the corner bed was Hassan's body; only a few scraps of flesh still clung to the bony fingers clutching the shredded sheet.

Simmons stumbled to the door, then froze. Over the rippling grass, through veils of shimmering heat, came the sound of moans growing steadily fainter.

The Dancing Dead of Shark Island

(British Isles—Ireland)

Just off the coast of Ireland lies the island that the locals call Shark Island, though its proper name is Inishark. One November night, Kathleen O'Connor, a young woman, trudged wearily along the road. She had been visiting a sickly relative and was now heading home. But the road was steep and rocky; she grew so tired that she sat down to rest. She shivered with more than the chill night air, for it was now the dread time that the islanders called "the hour of the dead."

She drew her shawl around her and closed her eyes for just a moment.

Then the sound of crunching gravel woke her. Instantly she opened her eyes and pressed her hand to her mouth to stop a startled cry. A pale young man was approaching her, though she could have sworn that the moonlit road had stretched empty before her when she had paused to rest only moments earlier.

"Don't be afraid," he said. His voice was gentle and his face was kind, though he seemed very sad.

"Indeed," said Kathleen, "there is something familiar about you."

"Look well at me," he answered, coming a step closer. "Now do you know me?"

"Yes, I know you now," she said, her voice dying away

to a frightened whisper. "You are young Brian, who was drowned last year when out fishing. Why are you here?"

"Look," he said, pointing to the side of a nearby hill. "That is why I have come."

Kathleen looked and saw a great company dancing to the sweet music of unseen pipes and drums. So graceful were their movements that they seemed to step and bow and spin as daintily as butterflies darting over blossoms.

The sight chilled her to the bone: for among those who danced so beautifully, she recognized all the people who had died on the island for as long as she could remember. Men, women, and children were clothed in white, and their faces were as pale as bone in the moonlight. So intent were they on the fairy music that they did not seem to notice the young woman who watched their revels in fascination and fright.

But when the music stopped, all the ghastly faces turned toward her. They raised bone-white hands, beckoning her to join them. They drifted toward her, stretching out their fingers as though they would take hold of her and drag her onto the hillside.

"Run for your life!" warned Brian's ghost. "If they bring you into the dance, you will never leave this company again."

Terrified for her soul, Kathleen turned to flee. But at that moment the hidden musicians again began to play. The unearthly music froze the unfortunate young woman where she stood trembling, as the smiling dancers gathered around her in a circle.

Brian, himself a thrall to the music, joined his hands with those of the other dancers. Around and around Kathleen they danced. The fairy musicians played madly. The ghosts spun faster and faster, until they became a

blur of whirling white in which she could no longer make out faces and forms.

Faster and still faster they swept around her. It made Kathleen dizzy to watch; the drums and pipes filled her ears and head with a frenzied throbbing. Her senses began to swirl; she grew faint. All at once she fell to the ground, unconscious.

She knew no more till she woke up the next morning in her own bed. Her brother, Kevin, anxious when she did not return, had gone out searching for her, found her in a faint, and brought her home.

But there was a weakness and a forgetfulness in her, so that she could not tell what had happened.

The herb doctor was sent for, and he tried every measure he could to save her. But in the end, he shook his head and whispered to Kevin, "She has got the fairy stroke, and nothing can heal her."

Indeed, though Kevin kept watch and prayed by Kathleen's bed, she grew steadily weaker.

Just as the moon rose that night, she turned her head a bit, as though listening. "Do you not hear it?" she asked.

Anxiously her brother listened. Sure enough, now he could hear soft music, infinitely sweet, unbearably sad, all around the house. When he stepped to the window to see who the musicians were, he saw nothing but the moonlit meadow behind the house.

The music stopped. There was a sigh from the bed, then silence. When he returned to Kathleen's bedside, Kevin found that she was dead.

Outside, the ghostly musicians struck up a mocking, lively tune. Mad with grief, Kevin flung himself out the door.

In the distance, for an instant, he saw Kathleen dancing away from their cottage, toward the moon-bright hills. She paused briefly to wave her pale hand at him; then she faded from his view as the music died away into silence.

"That I See, but This I Sew"

(British Isles—Scotland)

In the Scottish town of Beauly there was once a tailor, Sandy, who worked very hard; but he could not manage to put enough coins aside to get married.

It happened that the girl he loved, Flora, was also desired by Angus, who was a well-to-do farmer. But Flora wanted no part of Angus or his promises of riches and a grand house. She loved Sandy, and that was that. She would wait until he had put enough by for them to wed; and she put aside what she earned as a lady's maid so that she could marry her dearie all the sooner.

Now, there was the shell of a church nearby. During a feud between two powerful clans, it had been set on fire by the MacDonalds when it had been full of MacKenzies. Not a single MacKenzie had escaped. Since that time, the church was said to be haunted, and no one would go near it after sunset.

One day, Angus went to Sandy's tailor shop on the pretense of having a shirt mended. As Sandy plied his needle the two men chatted, and Angus brought the talk around to Sandy's lack of money to wed Flora.

"Just what would you be willing to do to get the money?" asked Angus.

"Anything!" answered Sandy.

"Well, then," said Angus slyly, "I'll give you what you

need if you'll spend as much of the night alone in the old church as it takes to sew me a new pair of trousers."

Now, Sandy knew all the stories about the ruined church being haunted by strange creatures. But his love for Flora was so strong that he agreed on the spot to what Angus proposed.

"Then," said Angus, "settle yourself in the church on the stroke of midnight. And when you've made the trousers, bring them to my door. I'll pay you for your sewing and your courage."

Angus sounded cheerful enough, but he secretly hoped that something terrible would happen to the tailor so that he would be rid of his rival for fair Flora's heart.

Shortly before midnight, the brave tailor arrived at the church. First he tested the door to be sure that it would close. Then he pried loose the latch on the inside of the door, leaving the outside latch as it was. This way, the door could be drawn shut from the outside, but not pulled open from the inside. He left the door ajar.

Inside, the fire-blackened stone walls were pierced with tall, narrow windows barely wide enough for a man's fist to fit through. Moonlight shone down through a hole where the center of the roof had fallen in. But it gave scant light. The tailor settled himself in one of the pews near the door, lit a tallow candle, and began to sew. The wavering flame sent shadows dancing all around him.

At first, all was quiet. Then, as the stroke of midnight tolled, the tailor gasped.

Leaning toward him out of the darkness was a great fleshless skull with grinning jaws and sockets without eyes. In a horrible, hoarse voice the bony jaws rasped, "See'st thou this big gray skull, O tailor?"

"That I see, but this I sew," replied the terrified little man as he bravely went on sewing.

"See'st thou this long, grizzled throat without food, O tailor?" demanded the thing as more of its ghastly self appeared.

"That I see, but this I sew," answered the tailor. Indeed, he was now sewing frantically.

"See'st thou this long, grizzled trunk without food, O tailor?" questioned the skull. It was drawing nearer, and Sandy could see more of the horrible shape now.

"That I see, but this I sew," said the tailor as well as he could through his chattering teeth.

"See'st thou this long, grizzled thigh without food, O tailor?" said the haunter, stepping fully into the candle-light.

"That I see, but this I sew," said Sandy. Indeed, he needed only three or four more stitches to complete the trousers.

But the skeletal thing was now towering over him. The moonlight, through the ruined roof, made its bones shine so brightly that Sandy could not look at it directly.

The tailor's hands were shaking so, he feared he could not finish his work.

"See'st thou this long, grizzled arm without food, O tailor?" growled the creature of bone and light. It raised its massive dead hand skyward with a loud rattle.

With trembling hands, the tailor took his last stitch and bit off the end of his thread.

At that instant, the thing stretched out its bony hand to seize him. Through its fleshless jaws it bellowed, "See'st thou this great, grizzled paw without food, O tailor?"

But Sandy, gripping the newly made trousers in his

hand, sprang to his feet and raced for the door of the church. Before he got through it the skeleton fingers caught at his leg, the nails raking the back of it painfully. Then Sandy was outside and had pulled the door closed behind him.

As he leaned against the sealed portal he heard the fumblings of the thing as, unable to find the missing latch, it began to scrape and scratch at the wood.

But the tailor was already racing for Angus's home.

Sandy presented himself to Angus, demanding payment of their wager. But Angus denied that Sandy had gone to the church. When Sandy showed the scratches on his leg, Angus claimed he had scraped himself with briars. They exchanged heated words. Finally a group of townsfolk, hearing the tailor's story and Angus's challenge, went to investigate the church.

They found deep scratches and dents that splintered the wood on the inside of the door and that could only have been made by the haunter Sandy had described.

So Angus was made to pay the tailor what he had promised, and was given the trousers that had cost him so dearly. Then Sandy and Flora were married and lived happily ever after. But to the end of his days, Sandy bore faint scars across the back of one leg, where the bony fingers of the thing had scraped his flesh.

La Guiablesse

(West Indies—Martinique)

It was a breezeless, cloudless noon, the hour of rest. In the dazzling light the hills seemed like blue smoke. Nothing stirred in the nearby fields of ripening cane, nor in the mysterious, vine-veiled woods beyond. The palms along the road held their heads still, as if listening and waiting for something.

Two young workers, Gabou and Fafa, were taking a break from their labors in the cane fields. They sat beside the road, fanning themselves with their wide straw hats.

As they watched, a woman came along the road, which led past them, over the mountain. She was young and very tall, with skin the color of polished ebony. She wore a high, white turban, an alabaster robe, and a white scarf draped across her shoulders. Her bare feet carried her swiftly and noiselessly.

Gabou was startled. He was sure she had appeared on the very stretch of empty road he had just been staring along. How could anyone have appeared so suddenly? he wondered.

But his friend Fafa just grinned and nudged him. Gabou answered with a smile. Neither had seen her before, but they both felt they could watch her forever: she moved with the grace of a dancer.

The lovely woman approached the two men, who stood and greeted her, *"Bonjou', Manzell."*

"Bonjou', Missie," she responded. She hardly glanced at Gabou. But she turned large, dark eyes upon Fafa. When she smiled at him, he felt wrapped in a blaze of black lightning.

"She makes me afraid!" whispered Gabou. Something in her look troubled him, though he could not say what.

"She does not make *me* afraid!" said Fafa. Boldly he put on his hat and followed the gently swaying figure, ignoring Gabou, who warned, "Fafa, have a care!"

But Fafa did not heed. The stranger slowed her pace, waiting for him. In a moment he was at her side. They climbed the mountain road together.

"Where are you going?" asked Fafa.

"As far as the River of the Lizard," she answered.

"But that is more than thirty kilometers!" he cried.

"What of that?" she said, gazing at him. "Do you want to come with me?"

There was such longing in her eyes, he could not resist. He heard the clang of the plantation bell calling him back to work. Far behind them, he saw a white-and-black speck in the sun: It was Gabou. For a moment he became confused. How had they walked so far in such a short time? he wondered. He thought of the overseer's anger, of the distance. Then he looked again into the woman's dark eyes and said, "*Oui,* I will go with you."

Then they both laughed like naughty children. She walked on, with Fafa striding beside her.

"What is your name?" asked Fafa.

"You must guess for yourself, my sweet."

Fafa disliked riddles, but he asked, "Is it Cendrine?"

"No, that's not it," she replied.

"Is it Vitaline?"

She shook her head.

All of his guesses—Aza, Nini, Maiyotte, Loulouze—were wrong.

Tiring of the game, she quickened her pace and began to sing,

> *Listen to this song of mine:*
> *I have traveled a long, long time.*
> *Love was gone; now it draws near.*
> *Will you be my love, my dear?*

Fafa had to walk faster to keep up. His thin cotton shirt grew soaked with sweat; he panted. Yet his companion's skin stayed dry; her easy steps and gentle breathing gave no hint of effort. At last she stopped and waited for him, still singing.

Fafa fanned himself with his hat. "Perhaps I should return," he said.

The smile left her face, replaced by a look of sadness. "Stay beside me," she said. "I will walk more slowly." Again Fafa was caught in the black lightning of her gaze.

As they continued, she moved at a gentler pace and became more friendly. The two talked loudly, laughed, and sang together.

They left the valley behind, climbing the steep road over the eastern peaks, through woods choked with creepers. As sunset approached, the sky deepened from lemon to orange above the distant lilac sea.

All at once the woman left the road to take a narrow path leading up through woods on their left. Fafa hesitated to follow, for the orange sun was rapidly sinking.

"Hurry!" she called. "This is the shortest way."

He obeyed, taking the path that zigzagged into shadow. Ahead, he could just glimpse her white turban

and white scarf. Then vines and boughs closed around him. The shadows of night mixed with the forest gloom. Huge fireflies sparkled like wind-tossed coals in the dark. He could not see her at all.

"Where are you?" he called, afraid.

"Here! Give me your hand!" she whispered.

The hand that guided Fafa through the shadows was cold. The woman walked with the sureness of one who knew the path by heart. Suddenly they broke from the forest, onto a ledge. From the ravine below their feet rose the sound of rushing water.

Her face was in shadow as she stood looking at the sky dotted with the first stars.

"Do you love me?" she murmured, her voice nearly drowned out by the sound of the hurrying stream.

"Oui, oui!" he cried. "You have my heart, my soul!"

She suddenly turned to him in the last faint red light of sunset, revealing the horror of her true face. She laughed hideously and taunted him, "Kiss me now!"

In that moment he knew her name—*La Guiablesse*—the goblin who haunted the sunlit mountain roads and who vanished by night. She took a step toward him. His brain reeled at the awfulness of what he saw. He stepped backward, and—

Falling, Fafa crashed to his death in the mountain torrent far below.

The Blood-Drawing Ghost

(*British Isles—Ireland*)

There was once a young man, John, in Ireland's County Cork, who was courting three girls at one time. He didn't know whether to make Mary or Peggy or Kate his wife. They all had sweet natures, and each was as pleasing to his eye as the other. His family was after him to choose one and marry, but he could not make up his mind.

Now, the churchyard in the town was said to be haunted. No one would go there after dark. As John walked past it one afternoon, he had a sudden thought. Pushing open the rusty gates, he went to the big tomb at the center. There he placed his blackthorn walking stick on the lintel, above the sealed doors.

That evening there was a gathering at a neighbor's house. As he expected, John found Mary and Peggy and Kate there. Kate asked right away, "Where is your blackthorn? Have you lost it?"

"I did not," said John. "I left it on the top of the tomb at the center of the churchyard. Whichever of you three will bring it to me this very moment, she's the woman I'll marry." He turned to his first sweetheart and asked, "Well, Mary, will you go for my stick?" he asked.

"Faith, and I will not," said Mary.

"Well, Peggy, will you go?" he asked his second love.

111

"Though it means losing you," said Peggy, "I'll not go."

"Well, Kate," said he to the third, "will you fetch my blackthorn? If you do, you're the one I'll marry."

"Sure, and I'll bring it," Kate said stoutly. And off she went.

The graveyard was three miles away, but Kate was a brawny girl with a fast stride, so she came to the place sooner rather than later. The moon lit the marble tomb at the center; she found the blackthorn with no problem.

But she had barely put her hand on it when a soft voice called from the vault, "Come and open the tomb for me."

Kate began to tremble and was very much afraid. But even as she tried to resist, a force compelled her to unwind the chain that sealed the double doors of the tomb.

Descending a short flight of steps, she found a casket resting upon a marble table.

"Take the lid off," commanded the voice from the casket.

Unable to help herself, she did as she was told. Inside lay the body of a man who had died months before. His eyes were open, but unmoving—yet somehow Kate felt them watching her. His dead lips were drawn slightly apart, and the voice came from between them, though the mouth moved not at all.

"Lift me out of here," the corpse commanded, "and take me on your back."

Afraid to refuse, she lifted the body partway up and turned around. Instantly the corpse threw his arm around her neck; his chest pressed against Kate's back and shoulders. She shook herself, hoping to shake free of

112

the thing. To her horror, she found she could not rid herself of the awful burden.

"Carry me *there*," the dead man whispered in her ear. He stretched his right arm out to point the way, but his left arm remained locked around her neck.

Thus guided, Kate carried the corpse out of the churchyard and along the stony road. The weight of the dead man grew heavier with each step. But Kate managed to reach the outskirts of town.

"Take me to the first house," whispered the dead man. She brought him to the door.

"Oh, we cannot go in here," said her burden. "Those people have holy water. Take me to the next house."

She went to the next house.

"We cannot go in there," said he, when she stopped in front of the door. "They have holy water as well."

He ordered her to a third house. Kate groaned when she saw that it was John's house, which he shared with his parents.

"Go in here," said the dead man. "There is no holy water in this place." Indeed, Kate knew that John and his family were not churchgoers and never kept holy water on hand to bless themselves.

Kate tried to hold back, but there was no help for it. She was under the devil's spell, and so they went in.

"Carry me to the room above," said he.

They went up to the room where John slept, unaware of his night visitors.

"Take the cup from beside the bed," said the dead man. "Hold it beneath his wrist."

Her hand trembling, Kate did as she had to do. With a fingernail that was like a claw, the dead man pierced the skin at John's wrist, drawing blood. This fell into the cup. When it was nearly full, the dead man touched his finger again to John's wrist. The wound closed, so that there was no sign of it. But it seemed to Kate that John's life had drained from him with his blood.

Before she could say a word, the dead man ordered, "Carry me downstairs."

In the kitchen, the corpse ordered Kate, "Put me in a chair at the table, fetch oatmeal and mix this blood with it in two bowls: one for me, another for you."

Kate got two bowls and put oatmeal in each, mixed this with blood from the cup, and brought two spoons. The dead man began to eat hungrily. Kate pretended to eat, hiding her portion in the napkin on her lap.

"Have you eaten your share?" asked the dead man.

"Sure, and my plate is empty, as you can see," said the young woman boldly.

"Come, now," said he. "Take me back to the church-yard."

"Oh, how can I do that? You are too great a load." She dreaded going back. And she was frantic to know if John still lived.

"What you have eaten has made you stronger," said the corpse. "You must take me back to my tomb before sunrise."

Again, she went against her will. But before she took up her burden, she hid the napkin and oatmeal behind the cupboard.

As she trudged the moonlit road, Kate asked, "What happened to the man whose blood you drew?"

"He'll die before the day is done," said the corpse. "The only cure would be to put three bits of the blood-ied oatmeal in his mouth. But not a speck was left in either bowl, so he'll soon rest near me in the church-yard."

Suddenly a cock crowed.

"Hurry!" urged the corpse. "I must be in my grave before dawn, and the cock has crowed once."

"Sure, and it was an owl you heard," said Kate. "There is time yet." With a great effort, she forced herself to walk more slowly.

A bit later, another cock crowed.

"Haste! Haste!" the corpse demanded. "I must be in my tomb before the first light of dawn."

"Sure, that was a dog baying at the moon," said Kate. And she walked more slowly still, though the strain nearly killed her.

"Faster!" the corpse ordered, raising his bony hand. "Cut across the field there. It will bring us to the churchyard sooner."

This time she was compelled to obey. As they went across the field, the corpse said, "This land was mine when I lived. Do you see those three piles of stones?"

"Indeed," said Kate.

"Underneath them is a pot of gold. Long I worked to save it," said he, "and little good it did me in that life or now."

Kate paused to stare at the heaps of stone.

"Don't stop now! Dawn is coming!" screeched the corpse. "And don't fill your head with thoughts of my gold. When we return, you will be as dead to the world as I am. The blood you ate has given you to me. You'll sleep at the foot of my coffin by day, and take me on my errands by night. Hurry!"

Though Kate made a final effort to slow down, they soon found themselves at the churchyard.

"Inside with us!" cried the corpse. "I feel the sun rising at my back."

The doors of the tomb were still ajar. The blackthorn that had caused Kate's troubles lay on the lintel above.

Just as she was about to enter the crypt, she said a prayer and found the strength to grab the walking stick and thrust it through the door handles, sealing the tomb.

At this, the corpse began to howl and curse and choke her with his powerful arms. She fought back, but her limbs felt weak as water. Suddenly a cock crowed a third time. With a shriek, the corpse fell away from her; and the gasping girl watched the dead man turn to steaming bones in the morning sunlight.

Grabbing the blackthorn, she raced toward the village. There she found John's house in an uproar, his parents having just waked to find him unconscious, nearly dead.

Quickly, Kate took the napkin she had hidden. She put three bits of the dead man's oatmeal in John's mouth. Instantly he woke and stretched, as if he had merely been sleeping.

He was astonished to see Kate in the room, with his parents peeping anxiously over her shoulder.

"Do you remember anything of last night?" asked Kate.

John said, "I recall nothing but falling asleep."

"Well and good," said Kate. Then she handed him the blackthorn, asking, "Now then, will you keep your promise?"

"Indeed," he said, "we'll be married as soon as you say the word."

Before the wedding, Kate took John to help her dig under the piles of stones in the field near the graveyard. There they found a pot of gold. After they were married, they had a pleasant life. But Kate insisted that John go to church with her each Sunday. And there was always holy water in the house so that they could bless themselves and their children.

Guests from Gibbet Island

(United States—from Washington Irving)

When New York was still a British colony, Ellis Island, in the harbor, was called Gibbet Island because pirates and mutineers were hanged there in chains, their bodies left for public viewing. Directly across the water from this grisly site was the Wild Goose Tavern, in the town of Communipaw.

The tavern keeper was a Dutchman, Yan Yost Vanderscamp, who had gone to sea as a young man. Word had it that he had become a pirate chief, and that his ill-gotten wealth allowed him to buy the tavern and decorate it lavishly. He employed a man named Pluto, also rumored to have been a pirate. No love was lost between them, but each endured the other for convenience.

Vanderscamp often played host to his former companions of the sea—a crew of rowdy devils. The townsfolk thought they were smugglers, but nothing could be proved. The British authorities were often summoned to stop the goings-on at the Wild Goose; but whenever they arrived, their quarry had returned to sea. And Vanderscamp grew richer with each visit from his friends.

At last the watchful British caught three of the suspected smugglers ashore, with a chest of Spanish gold pieces and jewels and bolts of silk. The three proclaimed their innocence, swearing that Vanderscamp had given them the goods.

117

No amount of knocking at the Wild Goose roused anyone. The door was locked; the shutters were drawn. Not a trace of Vanderscamp or Pluto could be found.

With no one to defend them, and the whole town accusing them, the three were straightaway hanged on Gibbet Island, in full sight of the tavern across the water.

Several days later, a much subdued Vanderscamp returned in a small boat oared by Pluto. He acted surprised to hear about the executions; in fact, he shuddered upon glancing across at the desolate island.

Afterward, what illegal business floated in and out of the Wild Goose was done secretly. Often, after sundown, Pluto would row his master out to a vessel riding the waves in the harbor, letting the darkness cloak their coming and going.

One night, Vanderscamp and Pluto were returning from such a visit. A distant rumble of thunder hinted at a gathering storm.

"Row faster, you good-for-nothing!" the tavern keeper bellowed, striking his man. He was in a foul mood, having taken a drop too much brandy on board, and having decided that the ship's captain had cheated him in their dealing.

Angry at this abuse, Pluto changed course so that the boat skirted the rocky shores of Gibbet Island. Vanderscamp, who had dozed off, was awakened by a creaking overhead. Lifting his head, he found himself looking at the bodies of his three former companions dangling on the gallows, their chains creaking and grinding as they slowly swung backward and forward in the wind.

"What do you mean pulling so close to the island, you blockhead!" cried Vanderscamp.

The other man grinned unpleasantly. "I should think

you'd be glad to see your old mates once more. You were never afraid of a living man, why be afraid of the dead?"

"Who's afraid?" blustered Vanderscamp. "I'd be glad to see my old friends, alive or dead, at the tavern anytime." He fished a bottle from under his cloak and waved it at the remains of his old partners. "Here's fair weather to you in the other world; and if you should visit this one again, I'd be happy to have you drop in for supper."

The rising wind shook and twisted the leathery flesh and bones, so that a sound like laughter seemed to come from them.

"Mind the storm!" yelled Vanderscamp.

Pluto rowed straight for home. But the storm caught them while they were still at sea. Rain fell in torrents, thunder crashed and pealed, and lightning blazed. It was midnight before they landed at Communipaw, dripping and shivering.

As he entered the Wild Goose, Vanderscamp was startled to hear the sounds of revelry from the big room overhead. Tired and muddled by his adventures that night, the tavern keeper turned on Pluto. "Why didn't you tell me we had guests tonight?"

"No one was due," grumbled Pluto. "The storm must have stranded some travelers."

"Well, I'll see to them—and maybe join them for a spot of ale to take the chill off me," Vanderscamp said.

Somewhat unsteadily, he climbed the steps. But when he threw open the door, there at a table, on which burned a light as blue as brimstone, sat the three corpses from Gibbet Island. They still had chains around their necks, and they clanked their cups together, singing:

> *Oh, three merry lads are we,*
> *Come home from over the sea;*

119

First on the sand, and then on the land,
And last on the gallows tree.

They suddenly broke off their song, turned their empty eye sockets toward Vanderscamp, and beckoned him to join them. When he remained frozen in place, they rose and started toward him.

Backing away in terror, Vanderscamp threw himself out the door, bellowing for Pluto. But he missed his footing on the landing place, and tumbled all the way down the stairs.

Days later, a search was made of the house; but it was found deserted—though drawers and chests had been emptied of anything valuable.

There was talk that Pluto had killed his master, hidden his body, and then robbed the house, escaping to sea. But Vanderscamp's boat was later found adrift, keel up, as if swamped by a wave. Shortly afterward, some fishermen spotted the body of the tavern keeper wedged among the rocks of Gibbet Island, just below the pirates' gallows.

How Vanderscamp met his end remained a mystery. The only witnesses were the three grinning skeletons in their chains. And what they knew, they told no living soul.

The Haunted House

(China)

The house in the Chinese city of Canton was old and had stood empty for more years than anyone could remember. It was so dark and mysterious-looking that many strange stories had grown up around it. One well-known tale said that anyone who entered the evil house would never come out again.

Now, there was a young man, Chao Yen, who was extremely inquisitive and who considered himself very brave. He came on a cloudy, moonless night to explore the abandoned house.

Carrying a lantern, he stepped through the perfect circle of a moon gate into the bamboo-choked courtyard beyond. Above the gate were carved characters reading, "The path and the bamboo lead one to the place of mystery."

This amused him. The builder of the house had already decided to give it a hint of otherworldliness. No wonder so many stories were told about the place.

A path of stepping-stones, overgrown with moss and weeds, led to the main entrance of the villa. A second round doorway framed a panel of rotting wood. On either side, pale walls stretched away into the shadows of a stand of bamboo. The walls were pierced with dark windows, each covered with lacy grillwork.

Eager to see what was inside, Chao Yen pushed open the door. It swung inward with a groan.

The room inside was filled with old-fashioned furniture, which cast weird shadows in the flickering lamplight. Rotting banners and scrolls hung on the walls, but dampness had made what was written or painted on them impossible to decipher. Layer upon layer of dust covered everything; clearly no one had been here for many years.

Suddenly Chao Yen stopped. Had he heard something? He listened carefully, but all he could hear was his own breathing.

He moved deeper into the house. Outside, rain began to fall, pattering on the roof tiles. Lightning flashed, and thunder roared and rattled the shutters.

Now Chao Yen entered a vast drawing room with a huge, carved teakwood desk and chair facing a window of square grillwork. Upon the desk was a scrap of dusty parchment with a fragment of a poem, as though the poet had been abruptly called away.

Setting his lantern on the desk and brushing away the worst of the dust, the young man read:

Daily I wander pleasantly in my garden,
There is a gate, but it is always closed.
In my empty rooms I enjoy the leisurely idle hours,
Shut away from the clamoring beyond the walls.
But it is getting dark, and the lovely day is vanishing.
Shadows fill my garden, flood my empty rooms.
Sighing wind in the bamboo, plashing water in the fountain,
Carry warnings of his approach.
Hark! In the stillness, I hear

There was nothing more. Chao Yen set the parchment down thoughtfully. The words had left him with a queer feeling of suspense, of something about to happen.

Suddenly he began to laugh at himself and his fears. A few shadows and some meaningless words and he was acting like a coward!

A rush of wind through the window extinguished the lantern's flame, startling him into silence. Then a vivid flash of lightning lit up the window. Beyond the grillwork, he saw a huge head—a man's head—on the body of a black dog. The creature was so big, it seemed to fill the window from side to side.

Darkness—blacker because it followed the blinding flash—closed in. Chao Yen waited, frozen in place. He listened, at first hearing only the rain. Then he heard the sound of unearthly breathing.

Another lightning flash. Now the monstrous thing was *inside* the room.

Chao Yen backed quietly away from the deep, ragged breathing, which marked the creature's whereabouts. At last he found himself pressed flat against the wall. Before he could begin edging toward the door, however, to his horror he felt the wall give way behind him.

He tumbled backward into a blackness even deeper than the night. There was a final flash of lightning that showed he was in a room littered with skulls and bones. All of them looked as if they had been chewed and splintered by massive jaws.

Then the creature pushed through the opening. Chao Yen heard its eager breathing; the secret chamber was filled with the reek of it; a massive paw raked his shoulder.

This was too much. The man whom nothing could frighten died of fear.

124

"Never Far from You"

(British Isles—England)

In a little English country church there is a stone inscribed, "In memory of the beloved bride and mistress of the family honor and estates, who was taken away by a sudden and untimely fate at the very time of her marriage celebration."

This is the story behind that sad inscription. . . .

Many years ago, a young woman, Alice, the daughter of a country parson, fell in love with Owen, the young lord of the nearby manor. Owen had come into his inheritance early, when his parents had died. And the young man was just as much in love with Alice. The handsome couple were often seen strolling hand in hand across the meadow, or riding side by side along a forest path.

They exchanged rings upon which were engraved the words "I will never be far from you, my love—be never far from me," above their intertwined initials.

Alice and Owen were equally fond of games. On the day of their wedding, they planned an afternoon of diversions. The bride, still in her gown of white lace, led her groom and their guests through all sorts of amusements: charades, cribbage, casino, and whist.

Finally Alice announced that the last game of the day would be hide-and-seek. One group, including the bride herself, would hide; it would be up to the groom and the rest to find them. When all those in hiding were located, the bridecake would be served, and the evening would be left to the young couple, who would depart for a honeymoon tour of Europe the next morning.

While the "seekers" counted to one hundred, the "hiders" scattered along the corridors and up the staircases and through all the chambers of the groom's vast mansion.

Alice, who knew the manor as well as she knew her father's house, went directly to the hidey-hole she had chosen long before. No one was around when she settled into her secret place. With a laugh, she thought how hard they would have to search to find her. In fact, she was sure she would be the last one found—and so would win the game. She was still laughing when something dealt her a blow on the head, knocking her senseless.

There was a faint *click*—then unending darkness.

Throughout the manor, the merriment of the seekers was matched by the laughter of those who were found. But as the late-afternoon shadows melted into evening, Owen began to grow uneasy. Everyone had been found but Alice. Because she knew every corner and cupboard in the manor, he was, at first, not too worried. But as time went on and the guests became concerned, he announced that the game was over.

Loudly calling Alice's name, the wedding party looked high and low. They searched the kitchens, peering into pantries filled with dishes and pots. They investigated each bedroom, looking under every bed and behind the curtains. The ballroom was searched; the dining hall; the library; the cloakroom. They shouted to Alice in the shadowed attic, where rows of dusty boxes and chests looked as if they had been undisturbed for a hundred years. They explored the cellar, filled with bric-a-brac that Lord Owen's ancestors had stored and forgotten. But Alice was nowhere to be found.

When the house had been combed top to bottom, Owen had his guests and servants widen the search to include the gardens, outbuildings, and nearby woods. With candles and torches and lanterns, they traced and retraced their steps. But they found no clue to Alice's whereabouts.

Where could she be? Poor Owen felt his heart would break.

Alice's father, the parson, was just as bewildered. Long after the other guests had left, he and Owen continued to search the manor from attic to cellar, calling Alice's name.

But she did not answer. She had vanished.

Rumors flew: Alice had run off with someone else . . . fearful of wifehood, she had entered a convent . . . she had been abducted by poachers when she hid in the woods. The only fact was: She was never seen again.

Owen never remarried. From time to time the parson would visit, only to find Owen holding the ring Alice had given him, his lips moving silently as he read the inscription: "I will never be far from you, my love—be never far from me." Then he would run his fingers over their intertwined initials.

In time, the parson departed this earth. Then Owen had no visitors. His loyal servants, whom he barely noticed, kept the manor from falling into ruin.

From dawn to dusk he wandered his estate, driven to the edge of madness, wondering what had become of his one true love.

And when he had grown old, he found himself in the attic one rainy day. The attic had become a refuge where he could be alone with his memories. He sat beside a small window, watching rain run in sheets down the dusty glass.

"If only I knew that your love was true, sweet Alice," Owen whispered, "then I could die happy." These days he felt that Death was another resident of the manor, though one who kept out of sight for the time being.

He wiped away a tear. Then something caught his eye: a tiny triangle of white lace, no bigger than a fingernail, caught between the lid and side of a trunk half hidden by several others.

Like a man in a dream, he went over to the trunk. It was closed; the latch was hooked over the swivel eye, sealing it. With trembling hands, the old man unfastened the latch and raised the lid.

There lay the mortal remains of Alice—now nothing more than a skeleton with yellowing bones the color of the rotting lace of her wedding gown. The trunk had been her tomb from the awful afternoon when its lid had fallen upon her head, knocking her out, while the latch had dropped into locked position.

In the dim attic light, her lover read aloud for the last time the words that were engraved in his heart as well as on the ring still circling her finger bone: "I will never be far from you, my love—be never far from me."

"We have never been far apart, my Alice," he murmured, "nor will we ever be."

So saying, he reached down, clasped her lifeless form to his chest, and died in her withered arms.

The Rose Elf

(Denmark—from Hans Christian Andersen)

In the midst of a garden grew a rose tree, and in the prettiest of all the roses lived a tiny elf. He was as well formed as a child, and had wings that reached from his shoulders to his feet. Each day he enjoyed the warm sunshine, flying from flower to flower and keeping company with the butterflies.

Humans rarely came to that corner of the garden. But one day, as he lay napping in the warm heart of his rose, the elf overheard two people talking. Peeping out between the blood-red petals, he saw a handsome young man and a beautiful lady sitting side by side on the bench shaded by his rose tree. From the way they held hands and gazed into each other's eyes, the elf could see that they loved each other deeply.

"We must part for a time," the man said. "Your brother does not like our engagement, and he plans to send me far away on business."

"It breaks my heart to think of you gone for so long," said the young woman.

"Don't be sad," her lover said. "This adventure promises rich rewards. When I return, I will bring enough for us to marry, whether your brother gives his blessing or not."

They kissed, and the girl wept. Then she picked the very rose that held the elf, kissed it, and pinned it to her lover's breast. She left then, whispering, "Farewell, Anthony, my love!"

In the rose, the tiny elf could hear Anthony's heart beating as the man walked through a grove of trees.

But suddenly another man blocked the path; the stranger's look was dark and threatening. The elf at once guessed this was the brother of the beautiful woman. Without warning, the newcomer drew out a dagger and stabbed Anthony. The murderer then cut off his victim's head and buried it beside the body in the soft earth under a linden tree. There he also hid the fatal dagger.

"You are gone and will soon be forgotten," said the evildoer. "And when my sister asks why you fail to return, I will tell her that young men are fickle and not to be trusted."

He scattered dry leaves over the disturbed earth with his foot, then left. But he was not alone: The little elf accompanied him, sitting in a dry, rolled-up linden leaf, which had fallen onto the man's hat as he dug the grave. The little elf shuddered with grief and anger at what he had seen.

When the evil man reached home, he took off his hat and went to see his sister, but found her asleep in her room. She stirred without waking and murmured, "Sweet Anthony." At this, her brother shook his hat at her sleeping form, as though to drive away her happy dreams. He did not notice the dry leaf falling from his hat onto the counterpane.

When he had gone, the elf slipped out of the leaf, placed himself at the sleeping woman's ear, and told her of the horrid murder. He described how her brother had buried Anthony beneath the linden tree.

"So that you will not think this is merely a dream," he

said, "when you awake you will find on your bed a withered leaf."

Soon she stirred, and found the leaf. Fearful, but determined to know the truth of her dream, she went to the linden tree. Brushing away the leaves and loose earth beneath the tree, she found her lover, and cried terribly. The elf was a witness to her grief, for he had ridden on a curl of her hair.

After weeping a long time, she took up Anthony's head, kissed his cold lips, and shook the earth from his hair.

"I will keep you near me," she said. She covered the body again with the earth and leaves; but she took the head, the rose she had pinned to her lover's coat, and the dagger.

In her room, she took a large flowerpot and placed in it the head and the dagger. She covered these with earth, and planted the rose in it. This was all she could do, for she could not bring herself to hand her brother over to the hangman.

The elf settled himself in the rose; and using his magic, he made the rose grow into a bush of blood-red blossoms. This gave some comfort to the young woman, who every day watered the wonderful plant with her tears. At first, her brother could not imagine why she wept over the flowerpot. When he came to understand that she was grieving for Anthony, he grew angry and cold. And when he realized that she had nothing but loathing for him, he went out of his way to avoid her.

Day after day, the girl would lean her head against the flowerpot, imagining she heard Anthony's gentle voice whispering to her. Sometimes she dozed, and the rose elf, at her ear, talked of sweet things and gave her restful dreams.

As she lived more in dreams and memories, her life faded. One day, her spirit joined her lover's in heaven.

When her brother discovered her lifeless body beside the flowerpot, he ordered his servants to arrange for her funeral—he would have no part in it. Then, because he fancied the splendid rosebush for himself, he lifted it to take it to his room. But the rose elf took a tiny, sharp thorn and stung the man in the hand, so that he dropped the flowerpot. It shattered, and those who had come to prepare the dead girl for burial saw the whitened skull. Then they realized that the brother was a murderer: His own dagger lay beside it.

The evildoer was sentenced to hang. And no one suspected that within the heart of the rosebush, which they planted on the young lovers' graves, there dwelled one who had punished a terrible crime.

The Wind Rider

(Poland)

In a small village in Poland long ago, a magician grew jealous of a young farmer named Andrusz. Both were in love with the same village maiden, Krystyna; but she was happily betrothed to the farmer. None of the magician's promises of wealth or power would turn her head.

So the older man went to Andrusz and offered him gold if he would give up Krystyna. But the farmer was greatly offended, and insulted the magician, and ordered him off his land.

The magician returned home in a rage. From that time on, he thought of nothing but revenging himself on Andrusz. One day, when the young peasant went into the meadow to rake hay, the evil magician went to the farmer's hut and stuck a new, sharp knife under the doorstop, saying, "I cut this fellow's bond with the earth and curse him to ride the storm wind forever."

At that moment a whirlwind arose in the field. It scattered the hay, then wrapped itself around the unfortunate Andrusz. The farmer tried in vain to resist the wind's pull. He struggled to cling to the hedges and trees with his hands. But in spite of his efforts, the storm wind pulled him up into the sky.

He spun around and around at the mercy of the winds of the upper air—helpless as a wisp of hay or cloud. He shouted himself hoarse, but no one saw him so high up. As the sun began to set, pangs of hunger set in, and cold chilled him to the bone. He looked with longing eyes at the smoke that curled from the chimneys of his village and carried the hint of warmth and supper cooking. He called even more loudly, and wept with frustration; but no one heard his cries or saw his tears.

Day after day he floated, like a hawk riding the winds, tormented by hunger and thirst. The breezes sometimes carried him north or south, east or west, but always returned him to the heights above his native village.

Every evening, the magician would come to the door of his hut and call up in a voice that only Andrusz could hear above the howling wind, "You will fly over this village forever. You will go on suffering, but never die. Such is my wrath."

Sometimes, at morning or noon, Andrusz would be whirled above the cottage in which his sweetheart dwelt. He would see her come out to hang the laundry or gather eggs from the henhouse, only to end up sitting on a bench, weeping into her apron. And sometimes he would see the magician, like a crow in his black robe, come to call and pat her shoulder and whisper in her ear. But always, fair Krystyna fled from him, back into the house.

Wretched Andrusz felt his lips grow hard; his face and hands became tough as leather; still he lived on, the plaything of the wind. Nor could he sleep, for the breezes chilled him and tumbled him about constantly.

Then one morning, when he felt like little more than a dried leaf, Andrusz again found himself above his sweetheart's cottage. Krystyna knelt in her garden, gathering cabbages.

136

He reached into his pocket and found the silver coin with which he had planned to buy a gift for Krystyna before the storm wind had gathered him up. He pressed it to his dry lips, and sent it spinning down. The sun glinted and gleamed off the coin as it turned end over end, falling to earth.

The coin landed in front of Krystyna. From above, Andrusz saw her pick it up in wonderment, then turn her eyes upward. Her hand shading her face, she scanned the sky. With the last of his strength, Andrusz waved his arms and kicked his legs.

For a despairing moment he thought she did not see him. Suddenly she stood up, spilling the cabbages in her apron, and waved back. Then she went running down the road.

Twisting like an acrobat, Andrusz was able to change position enough to see what she was about. Krystyna went right to the hut of the witch Zofia. Hope leapt in him: Andrusz knew there was no love lost between the witch and the magician who had sentenced him to living death. Perhaps Zofia would be willing to help him.

After a moment, Krystyna and Zofia came out from the hut. The hag looked up as the young woman pointed. Again, Andrusz waved, though he was so weary the effort nearly killed him.

The old woman began to weave a spell with her hands. Even from far above, the young man could see that her lips were moving, though no sound reached him.

Next the old woman began stretching out her left arm, then pulling it back, stretching out her right, pulling it back, then repeating these actions. She looked like a fisherman hauling in nets, or a child reeling in a kite. To his delight, Andrusz felt an invisible cord wrap itself around him. Slowly the old woman pulled him earthward.

137

When he finally came to earth, how eagerly the two lovers embraced—though Krystyna wept anew to see how badly off Andrusz was. She clasped his skinny hands to her lips and wet them with her kisses and her tears.

But Zofia came between them. "My power over the wind is strong," she told Andrusz, "but your enemy has the power of the blade. I can undo his spell, but it will take time. The moment he sees that you no longer ride the winds, he will recut the bonds that hold you to the earth."

First the witch took them into her hut. There she prepared a potion that restored the young man's strength. Then she told Krystyna, "Go and tell the magician that you have changed your mind. Buy us time to find the blade that is at the heart of this spell."

Eager to help her lover, Krystyna hurried to the magician's hut. Andrusz and Zofia headed for the farmer's cottage, which had stood empty all this time. After a long search, they found the knife under Andrusz's doorstep. "When this is placed under the wizard's own stoop," Zofia said, "the spell will turn back on him."

Andrusz went to the magician's hut; inside, he heard the voices of Krystyna and his enemy. When he had slipped the knife under the stoop, he boldly rapped on the door while Zofia stood nearby.

When the man answered, he was astonished to find Andrusz. In a moment Andrusz had knocked him to the ground. Then he called Krystyna to his side. Furious, the magician scrambled to his feet, muttering a spell. Krystyna clung to Andrusz, fearful of losing him a second time.

But Zofia suddenly undid her scarf and began to stroke her thick, dark hair. She chanted something the others could not hear. Although it was a calm day, such a storm

138

of wind arose that the magician's hut shivered. As Zofia stroked her hair faster and faster, the magician found himself whirling around and carried high into the air.

"Your enemy will trouble you no more," said the old woman as she retied her scarf. "He must suffer the torments that he meant for you."

So it was that Andrusz and Krystyna were married. And during the dancing and merriment that followed, one of the guests reported that he had seen the magician sailing through the air, over a lake far to the east. Before him and behind him flew ravens and crows, whose hoarse cries heralded the wicked magician's endless ride on the wind.

The Skull That Spoke

(Nigeria)

There was a clever young man, Kigbo, who was also lazy. He did not want to fish or hunt or grow yams. His words were honey-sweet, so he was always able to charm some food from his neighbors. But, though he was unwilling to work, he was greedy. He dreamed of becoming a rich man so that he could purchase cattle and wives, spend his days growing fat and contented, and always be respected by his tribe.

One day as Kigbo walked along a forest path, lost in dreams of gaining effortless wealth, he stumbled over a skull half buried in the soft earth. Annoyed, he struck at the skull with his staff, saying, "You foolish thing! Get out of my way!"

A second blow of his staff sent the skull rolling across the clearing.

To his amazement Kigbo heard the skull say, "Why do you treat me so? Why do you call me foolish?"

Though he was very much afraid, the young man said boldly, "You lie here forgotten, not buried by family or friends. Therefore, you must have been a person of no importance. And to have died poor, without wives and friends to bury your bones, means you were foolish, also."

"And you? Have you so many wives? Have you so much importance in your village?" asked the skull. And it

140

seemed to Kigbo that the fleshless thing was mocking him.

"I am clever," the young man boasted. "I will soon get for myself all the things I do not yet have. I will not die of foolishness, like you!"

"If I died of foolishness," replied the skull, "then you will soon die of your cleverness."

"Enough!" cried Kigbo. And he walked away. But as he walked, the young man began to get an idea of how to turn his chance meeting with the skull to his advantage.

Upon reaching his village, he went to the royal house and prostrated himself before the king.

The king demanded, "Why have you come before me?"

Kigbo answered, "I have found a skull that spoke to me. Surely such a wonder is a gift from the gods—a marvel worthy of a king."

At first, the king's wives and his counselors and his bodyguards laughed at Kigbo. But the king looked at the young man darkly and said, "Have you told this story in the hope that I would believe it, and therefore seem foolish in your eyes?" For the king was very much concerned with his own importance; to mock him was treason of the worst sort, and punishable by death.

But Kigbo said, "Upon my life, I promise you that I am speaking the truth."

"Then bring this skull, this gift of the gods, and set it before me," said the king. "If it says but one word, I will give you cowries enough to buy cattle and wives and heaps of yams. But if it fails to speak, I will have your head."

Filled with thoughts of all the riches that would soon be his, Kigbo retraced his steps into the forest. Soon he found the skull, and picked it up.

"Have a care, Kigbo!" the skull said. "If I died of my foolishness, then you will soon die of your cleverness."

Ignoring this warning, the young man hurried back to the royal house. There he prostrated himself, and set the skull at the king's feet. "Speak!" Kigbo commanded.

The skull spoke not a word.

"Speak, you foolish thing!" cried Kigbo.

Not a word came from the fleshless jaws.

Then Kigbo beat the skull with the end of his staff, but this had no better effect than his words.

The king, angry that Kigbo was playing a trick on him, made a sign to one of his bodyguards. Unmindful of this, Kigbo had picked up the skull and was shaking it.

The bodyguard's ax sliced through the air. Kigbo's head toppled from his now lifeless body. With another movement of his hand, the king signed to his servants to throw the young man's body and head, as well as the skull, into the jungle.

Head and skull rolled to a stop, facing each other in the forest shade.

"You foolish thing!" Kigbo yelled at the skull. "Look what you have done to me!"

But the skull only grinned and said, "It was your own cleverness that brought you here: for being too clever can be as fatal as being too foolish."

The Monster of Baylock

(British Isles—Ireland)

There is a curious legend that Ireland will never face the fire and brimstone of the Last Day; rather, the story goes, on the day before all other nations are delivered over to the destroying flame, Ireland will be devoured by a giant born of her own people.

The legend goes on to say that the devouring giant has already been born and is in hiding, waiting and longing for the day before the Last Day, when he can gulp and swallow the whole country that has been hiding him, alive, since ancient times.

This is the story of how that monster came to be. . . .

In times past, most people dwelt in Ireland's valleys and plains. Only a few lived in the mountains, where they had to fight for their living against wild beasts and against the ferns and bushes that were forever invading and choking their fields.

Now, it happened that a man and his wife lived in a little rough-and-tumble hut high up on the side of the Knockmealdowns. For years they longed for a child, but none was given them. So they went on working by themselves in that lonely place, where they only saw the occasional hunter or wood gatherer.

At last the woman had a son, and husband and wife rejoiced mightily on the day he was born.

143

A few days later, the woman left the baby snug in his cradle while she went out to milk the cow. Her husband had gone to gather wood for the fire. But when she returned with a jug of milk, the woman thought that the baby looked different. Leaning closer, she saw that he was growing. In a short time, he was too big to stay in the cradle, so he climbed out onto the floor. Then he took an oatcake, which was lying on the hearth, and swallowed it in one gulp, never minding that it was nearly as hot as a coal.

Not a sound did he make, but only looked around the place for more to eat. The woman had never heard the story of the giant who would devour the land before the Last Day, but she could see that something was greatly amiss.

Growing again, the child snatched up the jug of milk and downed it as though it were a thimbleful. After this, he caught hold of everything within reach that he could eat. All the while, he was growing bigger and bigger. Soon the crown of his head touched the roof of the cottage.

He grew again, and the rafters creaked. Quick as a wink, the monster child grabbed the cat hiding in the corner and swallowed it down. When he looked hungrily at the woman, she fled from the house with a shriek.

At most times there would have been no one to witness her distress. But this day, it happened that an old man was passing by. He was a wizard, and it was rumored that he could look into the future as well as cast powerful spells.

When he saw the woman racing down the path in fright, he called to her, "What is the matter?"

Before she could answer, the giant child stood up on legs as thick as tree trunks and tossed the roof of the hut aside as easily as a waking man throws off a blanket. Then he killed and gobbled up two bullocks in the pen beside the dwelling.

"Sure, that must be the giant who will swallow Ireland before the Last Day!" the wizard cried. "But the way he is growing, he will bring ruin upon us all before the appointed time."

"Can you do something to make him as he was?" asked the frantic woman.

"That is not in my power," said the wizard. "I cannot prevent what he was created to do. I can only keep him from doing it too soon."

The woman, caught between love of her child that had been, and fear of the monster that had come to be, began to weep and moan.

But the old man started to say spells and incantations, and to make charms and symbols from bits of twigs and grass that he pulled from the ground. Each time the giant, who was still growing, tried to seize the magician and the sobbing woman, the charms turned him away.

Three times the giant tried to snatch them, his hands as big as hayricks, his eyes blazing with hunger. Three times the spells kept him at bay, as if he had come up against an unseen wall.

At last the monstrous creature turned away and began to climb the steep path up the mountainside, behind the ruined cottage.

The wizard pursued him, still muttering secret words. All the while, the huge figure kept growing bigger and more terrifying. He was treading with heavy steps because of the spells that were upon him, but he was raging to devour the world. The fury in him made him awful to behold. The pounding of his heart against his ribs shook the mountains. His hair bristled thick and stiff and sharp

as spearheads. He roared like a hundred lions, so great was the anger in him.

Still, he thundered up the path, with the wizard following and the old woman coming also, for she must see how things came out.

Soon the giant reached the mountain lake of Baylock. And as the three of them straggled toward the shore, the wind began to rise and black clouds gathered over the hills.

When the monster planted his massive feet on the lakeshore, a wild blast of wind shrieked through the hills. A frightful, voracious vulture arose from the rocks and flew screaming over the water. The witches and goblins of the mountains rose up from cave and crevice; the destroying demons and ghosts of all who had died near that place filled the air. All were drawn, by the wizard's magic, to harry the monster.

Hidden behind a rock, the old woman watched wide-eyed as the wizard summoned a great, howling whirlwind down from the mountain peaks. This caught the giant and carried him out to the middle of the lake. There it dropped him.

In spite of his thrashing about, the giant soon began to sink. As he sank, the wind died away and the water became calm. Bird and banshee, ghost and goblin, fled back into hiding, and the silence of death hung over Baylock.

"Oh," wept the woman, "though he was a monster, he was once my babe. Now he's drowned and lost, never to return."

But the wizard said grimly, "The like of him is never drowned. But with the spells that are on him, he is chained to his fate. He must bide his time at the bottom of Baylock, until his bonds are loosened on the day before Judgment Day."

Ever after this, shepherds would say that, once a year, a whirlwind would blow through the peaks of the Knockmealdowns. And in the sound of it could be heard demons and ghosts screeching. The surface of the lake would churn. Then a thunderous voice would rise from the depths of the lake, asking, "Is it the day before the Last Day yet?"

When there was no answer, the voice would be stilled. Then, for another year, Ireland would be safe from the giant who is destined to devour the land on the day before the destruction of the world.

The New Mother

(British Isles—England)

When Queen Victoria ruled England there were two little sisters, whose real names are forgotten. But the older was nicknamed Blue-Eyes for the rich blue color of her eyes; her sister was called Red-Skirts, because she always wore dresses of that shade. They lived with their mother in a cottage in a seaside village. Their father was a sailor visiting faraway lands.

Their mother always told the sisters not to talk to strangers. But one day, as Blue-Eyes and Red-Skirts crossed the village square, they met an old woman sitting on a bench. She wore a black bonnet and white gloves, and her face was powdered as white as a ghost's. Her black skirt reached to the ground, and it crinkled and rustled like stiff tissue paper when she moved. Her eyes were hidden behind spectacles of thick, smoked glass. "Come here," she invited in a voice like pages turning in a very old book.

At first, the girls held back, remembering their mother's warning. But when the woman took a music box of carved and polished pearwood from her big, black silk purse, Blue-Eyes and Red-Skirts stepped closer to look.

The woman's gloved fingers worked stiffly as she turned a key in the back of the music box. When she

149

lifted the lid, tinkly music played, and a tiny carved boy and girl popped up and danced. The boy's painted mouth was sad; the little wooden girl had a single crystal teardrop under each eye; but Blue-Eyes and Red-Skirts were delighted. They laughed and clapped and begged the old woman to give them the music box.

"I will give it to you," she said, "but only if you are very naughty! Come back tomorrow and tell me how wicked you have been." Then the music wound down, and the wooden boy and girl stopped dancing, and the woman put the wonderful music box back into her purse.

"Now give me a kiss, and run on home," she said in her papery voice. The girls each kissed a cheek, finding that the woman's face powder tasted like dust. Then they ran home.

That evening, Blue-Eyes and Red-Skirts were awfully naughty. When their mother asked if they had spoken to anyone, the girls lied, saying nothing about the old woman in black skirts or her music box. Then they shouted and spilled their food and scribbled on their books and refused to go to bed. Their mother was very upset and said, "If you keep on being naughty, I will have to go away and leave you in the care of a new mother with glass eyes and a wooden tail."

But the little girls did not take her warning to heart. They thought only of the pearwood music box that would be their reward for such mischief making.

The next day, the sisters got up very early and hurried to the village square. There they met the old woman in black. Again she played the music box, and the tiny sad-faced boy and teary-eyed girl danced as before. "Did you do what you were supposed to?" the woman asked as soon as the music stopped.

"We were very naughty," Blue-Eyes cried.

"Yes," said Red-Skirts. "Can we have the music box now?"

"First tell me what you did," the woman demanded. She leaned forward with a sound like a door creaking.

Taking turns, the girls told what they had done.

"Oh, no," said the woman, "you were only a little naughty. You must be far worse than that. Now give me a kiss, and run along home." This time, her cheeks smelled like the parlor table when their mother polished it with lemon and beeswax.

All day long, Blue-Eyes and Red-Skirts were as naughty as they could be. They threw their teacups on the floor and tore their clothes and walked in the mud up to their knees and pulled up all the flowers in the garden and let the canary out of its cage, so that it flew away.

"Whatever has gotten into the both of you?" their mother asked. "Have you spoken to anyone?"

"Oh, no!" the two girls answered as one.

Then their mother said sadly, "Children, you must not be so naughty. If you do not stop, I shall have to go away, and then you will have a new mother with glass eyes and a wooden tail."

But Blue-Eyes and Red-Skirts thought she was only telling stories to make them obey, so they paid her no mind. The next day, they got up even earlier and ran to meet the mysterious woman in black.

But when they told her what they had done, she scolded them. "You haven't been nearly naughty enough. You must be *really* bad if you want any part of my music box. I will give you one last chance." They could not see her eyes behind her smoky spectacles, but her mouth was stern and no longer smiling. When they kissed her cheeks, the woman's skin felt dreadfully cold and hard.

Afraid of losing the music box, Blue-Eyes and Red-Skirts dashed home. This time they broke the chairs and smashed the china and tore their clothes to pieces and whipped the dog and even pinched their mother.

At last their mother said sadly, "Blue-Eyes and Red-Skirts, you have been so naughty that I will surely have to go away and leave you in the care of a new mother with glass eyes and a wooden tail."

Her daughters did not heed her. They only thought of the prize that would soon be theirs. "Tomorrow, when we have got the music box, we will be good again," they told each other.

The next morning, Blue-Eyes and Red-Skirts got up the earliest yet and went to meet the old woman. She patted the silent music box on her lap and asked, "Have you earned this?"

"Oh, yes!" the girls boasted. Then they eagerly told her all the wicked things they had done.

The old woman laughed and clapped her hands with a sound like two sticks hitting together. "Yes," she agreed, "you have been *really* naughty, and now your mother has gone far, far away to find your father. Soon you will have a new mother with glass eyes and a wooden tail—and the music box, too!"

But Blue-Eyes and Red-Skirts had grown frightened. The music box no longer mattered. They ran home, but they found that their mother was away. Hoping that she had merely gone to market, they mopped the floor and polished the silver and tried to undo their mischief. As

152

evening fell, they put the kettle on the fire to fix tea for their mother's homecoming.

While they waited for the water to boil, they heard a loud knocking at the door.

"Who is there?" called Blue-Eyes.

"Mother," a soft voice replied. "Open the door: I have forgotten my latchkey."

Something about the voice did not seem right to Blue-Eyes. But Red-Skirts cried, "We thought you had gone away!" She lifted the latch and opened the door before her sister could stop her.

There stood the old woman. She was so tall, her bonnet almost touched the top of the door, and her black skirts filled it from side to side. Her smoky spectacles were as big as saucers, and her black silk purse looked immense.

"Where is our mother?" asked Blue-Eyes.

"Because you were so naughty, your old mother had to go away," said the woman. "I am your new mother." She walked heavily into the cottage, growing taller with each step. Now the top of her bonnet reached to the rafters. From beneath her monstrous black skirts came a strange thumping noise.

"Run away!" Blue-Eyes yelled to Red-Skirts. "We will hide until our real mother comes home!"

But suddenly a wooden tail lashed out from under the black skirts and knocked them to the floor. When the new mother pulled off her spectacles, the flash of her glass eyes lit the room, so that Blue-Eyes and Red-Skirts clearly saw something round and dark coming for them. It was the mouth of the new mother's purse grown big enough to swallow them both.

———

One morning, two little boys playing in the village square met a funny old woman in black skirts and cloudy glasses who called them to her side. At first, they hung back, remembering how their mother had warned them against strangers. Then the woman opened her black silk purse and took out a pearwood music box. When she lifted the lid, tinkly music played, and two tiny carved girls—one with blue-bead eyes, one with dainty red skirts—popped up and danced. The boys were delighted.

They begged, "Can we have the music box?"

The woman smiled and asked, "How naughty can you be?"

Rokuro-Kubi

(Japan)

More than five hundred years ago there was a samurai named Kwairyo, who gave up the life of a warrior and put on the robes of a priest. But he kept alive within himself the heart of a samurai, and scorned danger. Those were lawless times, when a lone traveler was always in peril, even if he was a priest. But Kwairyo would go anywhere to preach the holy teachings of Buddha.

One evening, while Kwairyo was crossing the mountains of a remote province, darkness overtook him when he was still far from any village. He had resigned himself to sleeping under the stars, when a man came along the road, carrying an ax and a bundle of chopped wood.

"Good evening, sir," said the woodcutter, bowing to Kwairyo. "I am surprised to see a stranger on this road so late. Are you not afraid of things that haunt the dark?"

"My friend," Kwairyo responded cheerfully, "I am only a poor wandering priest, but I am not the least afraid of goblins. And I find lonesome places ideal for meditation."

"You must be a brave man indeed," the peasant responded. "But I can assure you this is a very dangerous region. Although my house is only a wretched hut, I beg you to come home with me at once. Alas, I have no food to offer you; but there is at least a roof to shelter you."

156

Kwairyo gratefully accepted his modest offer. So the woodcutter guided him away from the main road and up a narrow path through a mountain forest. After a long time, the priest found himself upon a cleared space at the top of a hill, with the moon shining overhead. Before him was a thatched cottage with paper lanterns glowing in each window.

First the woodcutter showed Kwairyo a shed behind the house. Here, bamboo pipes brought water from a nearby stream, so the men washed their feet. This done, they entered the cottage.

Inside, Kwairyo found two men and two women warming their hands at the fire pit in the center of the room. All bowed to the priest and greeted him respectfully. There followed some polite conversation; then the woodcutter showed Kwairyo to a little side room where a sleeping mat and pillow awaited him. Promising to pray for them to repay their hospitality, the priest retired.

The household settled into sleep, but Kwairyo read the holy *sutras* by the light of a paper lantern. As the hour grew late, he became thirsty. Remembering the clear-running water in the shed, he decided to go and get a drink.

To avoid disturbing the household, he gently pushed apart the sliding screens separating his room from the main chamber. By the light of his lantern, he saw five bodies upon sleeping mats—all headless!

At first, he thought that his hosts had been murdered. But a closer look showed no traces of violence or blood. Then he realized that this was a house of some Rokuro-Kubi, demonic creatures whose heads left their bodies to hunt food. He guessed that the heads had made their exit through the open smoke hole in the roof. He knew he was in great danger, since the creatures would devour any living thing—even a man.

Hearing no sound, Kwairyo unbarred the main door. He knew that moving the bodies would confuse and distract the creatures, so he dragged them out and hid them in a bamboo thicket. Then he hurried toward the stand of cedars at the head of the path. But when he entered the grove, he heard voices. Peering out from behind a tree trunk, he saw the heads bobbing and darting. They were eating worms and insects they found on the ground or in the trees.

"How fat that priest is!" cried the woodcutter's head. "How good he will taste! Though we cannot touch him when he is praying, he may have fallen asleep by now. Someone go and see."

The head of a young woman rose up and flitted batlike toward the cottage. After a few minutes she flew back, crying, "The priest is not there! And he has hidden our bodies!"

"We must find them," said the woodcutter, "or we will die. When I see that priest, I will kill him! I will tear him! I will devour him!" Suddenly the creature's eyes went wide, and he shouted to the others, "There he is, hiding behind a tree!"

Shrieking, the five heads flew at Kwairyo. But he had armed himself with a stout tree branch, and he struck the heads as they came at him. With tremendous blows, he knocked them aside. But the buffeting only seemed to anger them. They came for him again and again, their eyes burning, their sharp teeth *clack-clacking*. Though he wielded the branch as skillfully as he had once used a sword, the five heads were too much for him.

Two of the heads clamped their jaws on the branch and gnawed it to pieces. With snapping jaws, the three other heads dived at him. He chopped at them with the
158

sides of his hands, but each bit off a mouthful of his flesh. Desperate to find shelter from the snapping teeth, Kwairyo ran back toward the house, slapping and punching at his tormentors.

At the entrance, he swung around and punched the woodcutter in the face, slamming the head into the one immediately behind. Then he ducked inside the hut, pushing the door shut and barring it. He yanked on the cord that shut the smoke hole. But a moment later, he heard the screaming heads chewing at the oiled paper that covered the windows.

Kwairyo looked around for a weapon but could see nothing. In an alcove, he found piles of clothes, coins, and jewelry that the Rokuro-Kubi had taken from their victims. There were even a suit of armor and a sword.

Kwairyo snatched up the sword as ripping sounds, followed by screeches, warned him that the heads had chewed through the window coverings. To their dismay, they found that the priest had once again become a samurai. As the frenzied creatures flew at him, Kwairyo's sword cut them to ribbons.

At last, only the woodcutter's head was left. He had skillfully eluded the sword blade, managing to chew off several gobbets of Kwairyo's flesh. Though he was in terrible pain, Kwairyo stood his ground. When the howling Rokuro-Kubi rushed at his face, he waited until the last possible moment. Then his sword flashed. The upper half of the creature's head, its eyes filled with rage, struck the wall. The teeth from the lower half clamped on to the sleeve of Kwairyo's robe, biting as if the cloth were skin.

Instantly Kwairyo cut away the sleeve, then wrapped the snarling, snapping half-head in it and tied the bundle tight. When he had locked it in a wooden chest, he set fire to the cottage. Determined that no evil would remain to harm unwary travelers, the priest said a prayer that he hoped would bring the spirits of the Rokuro-Kubi eternal rest.

Dicey and Orpus

(United States—African American traditional)

Back in the old days, there was a girl named Dicey, who was born on a plantation. She was courted by a man named Jim Orpus, a wandering fiddle player who could make music like no one else on earth. Stories went around that when he played a tune, rabbits would come out to dance, and mules in the field would stop dead in the furrows and bray as if they were singing along. If he ever wanted a mess of fish, he'd just sit beside the creek and begin scratching away with his bow. Pretty soon fish were leaping into the air, then flopping on the ground around him. Then he'd set aside his fiddle, pick up what he needed, and throw the rest back.

Now Orpus was mighty sweet on Dicey, from the moment he saw her. She was shy at first. But when he played a soft, sweet tune for her, she would sing along. If she didn't know the song, she'd sing whatever words his music brought to mind; and Orpus seemed to like her made-up songs best of all. At first, she couldn't say how much she loved Orpus, but she sang her feelings clear enough. Soon they were married, all proper and regular.

Now, all this happened so long ago that the railroad was a brand-new, spick-and-span thing. Not knowing it was dangerous, Dicey sat down on the track one day, waiting for Orpus, because she thought she heard him fiddling in the far-far-away. But what she really heard was

162

the engine whistle. Before anyone could do anything, the engine came whistling and roaring around the bend, and smashed the poor girl.

After she was buried, Jim Orpus wept and wailed something terrible. He sat himself down on her grave, and he fiddled so sadly that folks for miles around thought their hearts were going to break.

Then he grew angry because Dicey had been taken away so sudden-like, and he couldn't do a thing about it. He began to fiddle up such anger that the mountains shook, and the trees splintered, and the ground trembled and crumbled underneath him. Orpus tumbled down into a big, old cave. He walked and he walked through the darkness toward a speck of light. Finally he reached the entrance to the Land of the Golden Slipper, the place where all the good folks go when they die.

When he got there, he found an angel who spread his wings and wouldn't let Jim Orpus pass. The angel said that only dead folks could go through the shining door into the Land of the Golden Slipper. Then Orpus carried on something fierce, saying he just had to get his Dicey back, or he might as well be dead.

At first, the angel wasn't having any part of this. But Orpus took up his fiddle and played such powerful sweet music that the angel began to weep and holler, and finally he said, "All right, I'll call Dicey here, and you can lead her back the way you came. But you've got to be sure you don't look back—not once—until you're both standing in the sunlight again. You're only going to get this one chance."

Well, Orpus agreed to this. He'd have agreed to anything to get his sweet Dicey back. So the angel told him, "Turn around. And don't you look back, or you'll be sorry."

163

The angel called Dicey's name. Pretty soon, Jim Orpus heard her voice behind him, asking what was going on. Though he didn't dare look, he knew that Dicey had seen him because she kept crying his name over and over and clapping her hands excitedly. Orpus heard the angel say how she could go back with Orpus, provided he didn't once look back at her till they were both up top again.

"You go first, Jim," said Dicey. "I'll follow."

He was so happy to be near her again, he almost turned around then and there. But he remembered what the angel had told him, so he kept looking ahead.

Back they went the way he had come. All the while, Orpus played a sweet tune, and Dicey sang along with him. At last they reached the place where her grave had crumbled down. He was all set to climb out, but he was so eager to see her, and they were so close to the finish, that his heart got the better of his head. He turned around.

For just a second he saw her sweet remembered face. Then she gave a terrible cry, and vanished like a comet back into the dark.

"Dicey!" Jim Orpus cried, and ran after her. But he couldn't spot the gleam that had led him to the golden gate earlier. And when he turned around, he couldn't see the place where the grave had crumbled. Not knowing what to do, he just began walking, calling Dicey's name over and over, and playing his fiddle to ease his misery.

The next day, when people looked for Jim Orpus, they didn't find him. Dirt had fallen into the big hole where Dicey's grave had been, and had filled it up.

Nobody ever saw Jim Orpus again.

But folks in those parts say that if you go into a cemetery where only black folks have been laid to rest, and press your ear to the ground, you can hear Jim Orpus's fiddle way down deep, as he searches for Dicey and the Land of the Golden Slipper.

Chips

(British Isles—from Charles Dickens)

There was once a shipwright named Chips. His father's name before him was Chips, and *his* father's name before *him* was Chips, so they were all Chipses. Each was a shipwright in his day.

Now Chips the father had sold himself to the Devil for an iron pot and a bushel of tenpenny nails and half a ton of copper and a rat that could speak; and Chips the grandfather had sold himself to the Devil for the same; and so the bargain had gone on in the family for a long, long time.

One day, while young Chips was alone in the dark hold of a ship hauled up for repairs, he heard someone say:

> A *lemon has pips*,
> *And a yard has ships*,
> *And* I'll *have Chips!*

Chips looked up and saw the Devil, with huge saucer eyes that struck sparks of blue fire. Over one of his arms, hanging by its handle, was an iron pot, and under that arm was a bushel of tenpenny nails, and under his other arm was half a ton of copper, and sitting on one of his shoulders was a rat that could speak. So the Devil said again:

167

> *A lemon has pips,*
> *And a yard has ships,*
> *And* I'll *have Chips!*

Chips didn't say a word; he just went on with his work.

"What are you doing, Chips?" asked the rat.

"I am putting in new planks where you and your gang have eaten the old away," said Chips.

But the rat said:

> *We'll eat the planking, old and new,*
> *We'll let in water to drown the crew,*
> *And when we do, we'll eat them, too.*

"That's as it may be," Chips said. He ignored the rat, but he couldn't keep his eyes off the copper and the nails, for these are a shipwright's delight.

"I see what you are looking at," said the Devil. "So take all that I carry and strike the bargain your father and grandfather did."

But Chips said, "I like the copper and I like the nails, and I don't mind the iron pot, but I don't like the rat."

"You can't have the rest without him," said the Devil.

"Very well," said Chips, afraid of losing the metal. They struck their bargain, and the Devil vanished, leaving Chips with the copper and the nails and the pot and the rat.

So Chips used the copper and nails, and he prospered. But he could not rid himself of the rat, which made its nest in the iron pot. Time and again he would try to sell the pot, but when the dealers saw the rat inside, that was the end of the matter. Once he dropped the pot with the sleeping rat off the pier, but both were back in his work space when he returned.

168

Chips had fallen in love with the corn chandler's daughter, but she would have nothing to do with him. For every time he spoke to her, the rat would suddenly peep out from under his collar or from his pocket, and the young woman would walk away in disgust.

One day, while the rat lay sleeping in the iron pot, a desperate Chips tipped a kettle of scalding pitch into the pot, filling it full. He watched until it cooled and hardened; then he got the smelters to put the pot into their hottest furnace. The pot melted and ran away in white-hot streams, but when the furnace cooled and the door was raised, out scampered the rat, just the same as ever. It looked at Chips, and said with a jeer:

A lemon has pips,
And a yard has ships,
And I'll *have Chips!*

Then it scurried away. For a long time, Chips saw no more of the creature. He began to hope it was gone for good. He even became engaged to the corn chandler's daughter.

But one evening, as he left the dockyards to go home, he reached into his pocket and found a rat. Not the one that could speak, but an everyday shipyard rat. In his hat, he found another. And in the sleeves of his coat, two more!

From that time on, he was never free of rats. They climbed up his legs at work. They sat on his tools when he used them. They got into his lodging and his bed, into his teapot and his boots. When he brushed himself free of them to present the corn chandler's daughter with a sewing box he had made for her, a large, fat rat jumped

169

out of it and clung to the girl's skirt. And that was the end of Chips's engagement.

Soon after this, he lost his job at the shipyard because of the plague of rats that followed him everywhere. Even when he was penniless, the rats remained his steadfast companions.

One night, driven nearly mad, he dove into the water and swam for a ship that was just setting sail. When he was hauled on board, dripping and shivering, he offered to work to earn his passage to the West Indies, where the ship was bound.

On they sailed, and with each passing league, Chips felt more hopeful, though he was made to do the meanest work. Once, the captain ordered Chips lowered on a rope, to scrape the salt from the ship's carved figure-head. But when Chips was partway down, he discovered that the rat that could speak had gnawed a hole as big as a saucer in the figure's wooden chest.

The rat winked at him and said:

> We've eaten all the timbers through,
> We'll let in water and drown the crew,
> And when we do, we'll eat them, too.

In the dark space behind the rat that could speak, Chips could make out the red eyes and white teeth of countless other rats. Bellowing and tugging on the rope, he had himself hauled back on deck. Then, pushing aside the sailors, who thought he had gone mad, he shouted at the captain, "The rats! They're nibbling us away! We're doomed, unless we make for the nearest port! There is dust and hollowness where solid oak should be! A rat is nibbling a grave for every man on board!"

But the captain also thought Chips a madman. He had Chips clapped in irons and chained in the hold. There Chips continued to shout his unheeded warnings, pausing only to put his ear to the wall behind him, listening to the gnawing and nibbling within.

When the ship's bell sounded midnight, the first snout chewed through the wall beside Chips. Water began to leak from the hole. Then an unstoppable torrent gushed in, and the ship went down with every living soul.

What the rats (being water rats) left of Chips floated to shore, and sitting on him was an immense rat, laughing, which dived under the waves when the corpse touched land, and never came up.

There was a lot of seaweed clinging to the remains of Chips. And for a long time, the story lingered that thirteen bits of this seaweed, when dried and burned in a fire, would go off with sounds like these thirteen words:

A lemon has pips,
And a yard has ships,
And I've *got Chips!*

The Skeleton's Revenge

(Mexico)

In the seventeenth century, in the village of Santiago near Mexico City, there lived a gentle old priest named Don Juan de Nava, who was much beloved by his neighbors. He labored selflessly to settle arguments, guide young people, help the poor, and teach the ways of God to rich and poor alike.

At the time, Mexico City was situated on a large island surrounded by lakes. A raised road of packed earth, called a causeway, linked Santiago with the capital. Just outside the village, a water-filled ditch cut across the road. This broad gap was spanned by an old stone bridge close to the simple house of Padre Juan.

Here the old priest lived with his niece, Margarita, whose parents had died. She was a young lady of virtue, intelligence, and great beauty. And she was courted by all the young men of Santiago and Mexico City.

As it happened, a wealthy young nobleman from the city, Don Duarte, fell madly in love with Margarita. In those days, courtships followed many rules; so the young couple could only exchange soft words or roses or little gifts through the iron grating of a window in Padre Juan's house. Sometimes Don Duarte strummed a guitar as he sang songs beneath Margarita's balcony.

As he watched the growing affection between the two, Padre Juan took upon himself a father's responsibility for his orphaned niece. Putting on his best cassock and sandals, he walked to Mexico City to learn what he could about Don Duarte. He wanted to be sure that the man would make a proper husband.

But what he learned greatly upset Padre Juan. One and all told him that Don Duarte lived a shameless, wild life, mocked the laws of God and man, and had broken the hearts of many women—from serving girls to the daughters of the finest families. Heavyhearted, Padre Juan returned home, where he told his niece that she must have nothing more to do with the young man.

That very night, through her window grille, the weeping Margarita told her suitor that her uncle would not allow them to marry. At this, Don Duarte made such dreadful threats against her uncle that she covered her ears and ran to her bedroom.

Now, Don Duarte was not a man to give up easily, and he was determined to wed the lovely Margarita. So one night, he waited on the old stone bridge. When Padre Juan returned from visiting an ailing farmer, the young man begged the priest to talk with him. The priest, always anxious to believe that there was hope for every sinner, listened as the young man promised to mend his ways. He swore that he would prove a loving, respectable husband, if only the priest would permit him to wed Margarita.

But Padre Juan, who had seen the best and worst in the human heart, felt that the words, which came so easily to the young man, were lies. He sensed that there was no honesty, no love, no change in Don Duarte. Even Padre

Juan's generous heart recoiled from what he saw of the man's true nature. Politely but firmly, the priest refused Don Duarte's pleading.

Seeing that his appeal had failed, and enraged to think that he might lose the woman he had set his heart upon, Don Duarte drew his dagger and plunged it almost to the hilt into the skull of Padre Juan. Without a sound, the old priest fell dead upon the stones of the bridge.

Because the dagger, with its ornate handle, would easily be recognized as his, Don Duarte began to pull on it. But no matter how hard he tugged, he could not budge the blade. Frantic to hide his crime, he tossed the body, with the dagger still in place, off the bridge and into the water. Then he fled into the night.

The disappearance of Padre Juan caused a great stir throughout the Valley of Mexico. Santiago and the countryside were searched, but no trace of the priest was found.

Don Duarte, knowing that he could not approach Margarita during the time of mourning, gave himself over even more completely to his reckless, wicked life. But thoughts of Margarita inflamed him. He decided he would visit her. If he could not persuade her to run away with him, he would carry her off.

Don Duarte returned to Santiago on a stormy night. Heavy clouds were split by bursts of lightning. Rain began to fall in great drops as Don Duarte, his cloak wrapped tightly about him, splashed along the rain-slick causeway.

When he reached the stone bridge, he heard a strange scraping noise ahead of him. But try as he might, he could see nothing in the rain-swept darkness. Then a flash of lightning revealed a tall skeleton, wrapped in a

175

torn and soaked cassock, coming toward him step by step. Sticking out of the skull at a grotesque angle was the murderer's now-rusty dagger.

Don Duarte turned to flee, but it was too late.

At dawn, a farmer crossing the bridge on his way to market found a gruesome sight. Sprawled in a puddle was the body of Don Duarte, an expression of absolute terror on his face. Beside his body, its bony hands locked around his throat, was a weather-beaten skeleton, still clothed in a tattered cassock. A rusty dagger jutted out of its skull, and its jaws were frozen in a horrible grin.

Lullaby

(British Isles—England)

Colonel Ewart was a man who detested riding trains and omnibuses, primarily because he was unhappy sharing space with strangers. Strangers wanted to chat, to ask rude questions, to tell him things that he hadn't the least desire to hear.

When business required him to make a trip, he would plan roundabout routes on unpopular trains in the hope that they would be reasonably empty. He didn't mind the extra time, as long as he could sit and read his paper without interruption.

Having plotted out just such a rail trip from Carlisle to London, the old soldier congratulated himself when the porter showed him to an empty compartment. His luggage stowed, the colonel happily unfolded his newspaper and settled in for a good read. But he kept one eye anxiously on the door, for fear some late-arriving passenger would intrude. With relief, he heard the whistle blow and felt the train moving out of Carlisle Station.

The warmth of the day and the rocking of the train soon lulled the colonel to sleep.

He awoke with a start as the newspaper slid from his lap, hitting the floor with a thump. As he bent to pick it up, he found, to his annoyance, that he was no longer alone. On the seat opposite sat a woman. She seemed well

178

dressed, though her clothes were a bit old-fashioned. Her face was heavily veiled, and she had a shawl draped over her shoulders, which fell down across her forearms. She seemed not to notice him at all.

Glancing at his watch, the colonel saw that he had slept for almost an hour. He had been so deeply asleep, he had not even noticed the train stopping to pick up this passenger.

He nodded to the lady politely, then returned to his paper. His companion did not nod back, or even turn her head toward him. She just sat, hunched forward, looking down. Then she began to rock gently, her arms and the draped shawl hiding what she was cradling. Softly she crooned a lullaby:

> *Hush, hush, my sweet, my dearest, my love,*
> *Hush, hush, my treasure, my angel, my dove.*

She was traveling with an infant, the colonel decided. She just kept singing the same bit of lullaby over and over, rocking ever so slightly. Something about her made him uneasy. At last he decided that he must speak to her. The silence between them had become oppressive.

"Madam," he began.

She did not look up.

"Madam," he repeated, edging forward a bit.

She made no direct reply, but stopped her humming. Then she turned toward him, still hiding what lay in her arms. Through the veil, the colonel could see a pale face, and eyes that looked almost hostile. Now she glanced down at her lap and hugged the unseen bundle protectively. She glared across at him with the fierceness of a she-lion protecting a cub.

Astonished, he sat back and buried his face in his pa-

179

per. From across the compartment came the monotonous lullaby.

Finally Colonel Ewart found himself overwhelmed with curiosity about the unseen infant she was hugging so jealously. Setting his paper aside, he stood up and peered across at the woman, determined to get at least a glimpse of the child.

At that moment three things happened. The woman's mouth opened in a scream of soundless horror; her arms rose to defend what lay on her lap; and a deafening crash shook the train, throwing the colonel to the floor.

For a few minutes he lay still, collecting his thoughts and assuring himself that he was merely bruised. His luggage had spilled from the overhead rack and lay pell-mell.

Concerned for the woman and her infant, Colonel Ewart turned to check on them. They were gone; the bench was empty. He heard shouts from outside the stopped train and assumed that the woman had fled the compartment in fear right after the impact.

The train had not derailed, and Colonel Ewart began to put his luggage in order. When he asked a conductor what had happened, the man said there had been a collision with a van of some sort. The damage was minor, and injuries were few.

When the colonel asked about the woman, the conductor gave him a curious look. "I passed your compartment shortly before the accident. You were alone."

"Nonsense!" exclaimed the old soldier. "I most certainly didn't imagine the woman and her baby."

"A *baby*, sir?" said the man, clearly more confused.

"Well, I didn't actually *see* it. I was just about to get a peek at it when the crash came. But she was certainly singing a lullaby to *something*."

The conductor's face went quite pale. "She's come back, then," he said in a hushed voice.

"What do you mean? Does she travel on this train often?"

"Only when there's going to be a mishap. She's a ghost, you see," the conductor said. Before the colonel could respond, the man continued: "Years ago, some newlyweds were traveling to London for their honeymoon on this train. They had this compartment to themselves. But we could pretty well guess what happened."

"Well?" said Colonel Ewart.

"The young man must have been leaning out the window when the train was at full steam. Another train went past, going the other way. There must have been a spike of sharp wire or something else sticking out. Cut his head clean off, sir."

Colonel Ewart suddenly felt queasy.

"The conductor found her, rocking and singing to the body. She'd pulled the . . . er . . . shoulders off the floor into her lap. A terrible sight she was—gone mad as a hatter. When they came to take her away, she put up a fight. Said she had to go back and find her husband's head. I heard she died soon after."

"Did they ever find his head?" the colonel asked.

"Never did."

Remembering the bundle cradled in his strange companion's lap, the old soldier said with a shudder, "I think the poor soul has somehow found what was lost all those years ago."

Death and the Two Friends

(United States—South Carolina)

There were once two friends who lived together in a cabin north of Charleston. George Heyward was a big, strong, able man. His companion, Aaron Dinkins, was small and weak. He had been felled with a fever the year before, and thereafter did not know a single healthy day, as the illness wore him down. He was so full of pain and restlessness that he could not sleep at night. He moaned and groaned and muttered over and over, "I wish I was dead."

For a long time George had compassion for his friend. But after a time, the strong man, who had never known a sick day in his life, grew weary of Aaron's complaining day and night. Though he fought it, he could feel anger building up inside him.

One night, George's feverish friend grew more restless than usual. Aaron turned and twisted, but he could find no peace from the burning fever and his aching joints. "Oh," he cried in misery, "I wish I was dead!"

George, who had been waked from a sound sleep by Aaron's cry, snapped at him, "You wish you were dead? Then why, in heaven's name, don't you just die and be done with it, instead of carrying on and never leaving me a minute's peace? Why don't you call Death to come get you, and put an end to all your wretchedness?"

Aaron, at the end of his strength, said, "All right; I'll call him. I don't want to live much, anyway."

He hauled himself upright on the bed, swung his legs over the edge, and staggered to the door. He fumbled it open and called, "Death! Oh, Death! Come and claim me." But his voice was very weak and feeble—hardly more than a whisper.

Now Death was way down yonder at the crossroads, sitting on a stump, waiting for someone to hail him. But Death could not hear what the sickly man whispered, Aaron's voice was so puny and uncertain.

The two men in the cabin sat and listened. When Death made no answer, George said to Aaron, "He didn't hear you holler. Holler again—only holler *loud* this time."

So the fevered man called again, "Death! Oh, Death! I'm waiting for you!" But his voice had grown even weaker and fainter from the effort.

"Shuh!" said his strong friend in disgust. "That's no way to call Death. You don't holler louder than a busted cockroach. Let somebody holler as can holler!"

With that, George went to the door and bellowed loud and bold, at the top of his voice, "DEATH! OH, DEATH!"

Before the big man could turn or say "Oomph!" something dark and dismal and grinning without mirth clamped a heavy hand on his shoulder.

George twisted around and said, "Who are you, and what do you want?"

"I am Death," said the dreary thing. "You called me, and I came."

George had no chance to say another word: Death took him into the dark, and left the ill and puny man

184

lying in his bed. In the morning, Aaron's fever broke, and he lasted many more years.

People would look at Aaron and recollect George Heyward, dead and buried for many years. Then they would shake their heads and say, "Death has a singular sense of humor, letting a weak and sickly man outlive a strong one."

But Aaron, who counted himself blessed to have seen Death's grin without feeling his touch, gave himself fully to the business of living. No matter how bad things might get for him, he resolved to hold fast until Death called *him*.

Forest Ghosts

(France)

In seventeenth-century France, a powerful count built a château amid densely wooded hills. He eagerly looked forward to spending leisurely hours at his forest retreat, away from his duties at the king's court.

In time, the count married. His new bride, Heloise, appreciated the grand house and surrounding gardens. But the forest gloom disturbed her. The trees pressed together, blocking out the sun, so that she felt as if she lived in a perpetual green twilight. Through open windows came waves of forest damp—and the ever present scent of mold.

One summer afternoon, Heloise lay down on a couch near one of the open terrace windows, fanning herself.

Suddenly a curious figure emerged from the grove of trees opposite the window. At first, it looked like a swaying branch of moss-covered oak. But as it approached Heloise, the strange shape resolved into the form of a woman. Her hands, face, and long, flowing robe were all forest green. A faint fragrance of ferns and mold clung to her.

Like one in a dream, the countess asked, "What do you want?"

"This is my forest," said the green woman. "I let your husband build this place because he loves and respects

186

the wildwood. He forbids visitors to hunt the animals in my care. Promise me that you will respect the forest the same way, and I will grant you one wish.''

Certain that she was having a waking dream, Heloise gave her promise. Then she said, "I wish to have a son, since that would please my husband.''

The green woman nodded. Then she became transparent and faded from view. Heloise felt herself drifting off to sleep.

When she awoke, she dismissed the matter as a dream. But she recalled the woman's promise when she learned she was going to have a baby. When Heloise presented her husband with a son, whom they named Henri, their joy was perfect. The countess even found herself appreciating the woodland estate more and more.

Once or twice, while riding in the carriage, holding her infant son, she thought she glimpsed the strange figure in green robes in the forest shadows. But the shape quickly vanished. When she questioned others, they said they had seen nothing. They suggested she had imagined the strange shape. In time, the countess came to agree with them.

Her real concern was her son, Henri. He loved the place; and when he was old enough, he spent hours playing among the forest trees. By the age of ten, he was as tall and big-boned as a lad of eighteen, with enormous hands and feet. When the days were warm, he ran half naked in the forest, where he built huts of oak boughs roofed with fern fronds, and lived like a wild creature.

When the boy was nineteen, the count died. The countess, whose health was frail, had long since abandoned her hopes of presenting her odd son to the king and court. Though she loved Henri deeply, she would often sigh as she watched him set off into the forest, running and bounding like a deer.

When he turned twenty-one, Henri suddenly announced to his mother that he was going to make the château into a hunting lodge. Heloise could not imagine what had put him at odds with the forest he once loved. He said only that he had a debt to pay a stag—a creature he called Satan—which had tried to gore him with its antlers.

Remembering the waking dream she had had before Henri's birth, and the words of the forest woman, Heloise tried to change her son's mind. But Henri was resolute. Soon the château was roused from its green drowsiness as huntsmen of all ages came to enjoy the sport. New stables were built to house a hundred horses. Every morning, the hounds and huntsmen, with Henri at their head, rode out in hopes of running a stag to earth.

The countess watched with growing unease, though she told herself that her fears were merely born of dreams and fancies.

That autumn, when mother and son were alone in the château, Henri suddenly announced that he was riding out by himself. Filled with foreboding, the countess waited anxiously for her son's return.

Near evening, from far down the tunnel of trees that led to the main gates, there came the shrill cry of a beast in agony. Then silence. Then a second cry—but this time, it sounded like a human in distress.

Heloise clutched the curtain as she saw a dark, massive shape emerge painfully from the shadows. At first, she thought it was a wounded stag bearing magnificent antlers. But as the injured creature drew closer, she saw, to her horror, that it was her son, Henri. He was antlered and shaggy, a creature neither animal nor human.

Henri was bleeding from a gash at his temple. His mother immediately shouted for the servants. At first, they would not come near. But the countess ordered them with such fierceness that at last they carried him upstairs.

Day and night, Heloise nursed her son. His body was human, but covered with long red-brown hair. His head was that of a full-grown stag—long snout, black muzzle, antlers like brown ivory sprouting from his temples. For a long time, he could not speak. But the torment in his violet-brown eyes nearly broke his mother's heart. At last he was strong enough to signal for writing paper. Still unable to talk, he wrote out what had befallen him.

On the fateful day, he had spotted the stag he called Satan. This time, he had refused to abandon the chase until he had run his quarry to earth. At last the winded animal had collapsed in a glade. Just as Henri hurled his spear, a woman dressed in green appeared in front of the stag. The spear sped right through her nearly transparent shape, which melted away so quickly, Henri thought it a trick of the light.

His spear buried itself in the stag's flank. But when the young man leapt from his saddle to finish the animal with a knife stroke, the stag suddenly gashed him with its antler before it died. In that moment, Henri felt himself changing. His horse, startled by the sight of its antlered master, galloped away. And the dazed youth was forced to return to the château on foot.

As the days passed, Henri grew stronger. But he also became more restive, pacing his room, smashing the mirror, crying out in a voice at once human and animal, which left the servants cowering in terror.

One evening, the countess heard terrifying sounds of breaking and ripping and snorting coming from Henri's room. Afraid that he was having a fit, she summoned her strongest manservants. When they opened his door, they found the room in ruins. At that instant, the strange, antlered creature that had been Henri burst through the window and leapt onto the roof like a panicked animal. Losing his footing, he plunged with a heavy sound to the courtyard below.

As his mother and servants knelt beside the dying man, they were astonished to see the tall figure of the green woman walking slowly from the forest shadows.

She gazed down at Henri's broken shape and said, "This forest is mine. The animals who live here are my charges. You, Henri, hunted and killed my stag. You violated the wildwood, and so you are paying for your deed."

She turned away, but the countess begged her, "Please, lady. You gave him to me; do not take him from me now."

"I cannot change what must be," said the green woman. "But I will give you some other wish."

"Then let me see my son as my son," said the countess.

The forest woman did not move, but what looked like green fire reached out from her to bathe the young man's body. The antlers faded to nothing. The matted hair became smooth skin. Snout and muzzle reshaped themselves into handsome features.

For a moment mother and son gazed tearfully at each other. The forest woman returned to the shadows with-
190

out a glance backward to where the mother embraced her dead son.

The countess died a short time later. And for many years after this, those who visited the château spoke of seeing, on rare occasions, a form, antlered like a stag, that would suddenly turn into the shape of a handsome man, only to melt the next instant into the green forest shadows.

A Carolina Banshee

(United States—North Carolina)

Years ago, a mill stood on the banks of the Tar River in North Carolina. Though it has long since fallen into ruin, leaving no trace, the site is haunted by a banshee. On August nights, when mist floats above the river and the rain crow warns of rain, a banshee's ghastly moans and shrieks rise from the reedy riverbanks, through the oaks, to fill the sky. Her cries are a reminder of tragic events that echo down to this day. . . .

During the Revolutionary War, David Warner ran the Tar River mill. A patriot who hated the English, he used his mill to grind wheat and corn for the American army. From dawn until far into the night, the water-driven mill wheel ground away.

Late one August afternoon, Warner stood in the doorway of the mill, absently brushing flour dust from his dark hair and beard. From far down the road, he heard the *thud-thud* of galloping horses. Before the riders came into view, a runner burst from the underbrush.

"The British are on their way here!" the man panted. "They know you for a rebel, and they plan to kill you."

Warner flexed his muscular arms. "I'll send them packing."

"You can't fight a whole army single-handed," protested the runner. Then he hurried off to warn others in the area.

But Warner went back to his work. He was sacking meal when six British soldiers appeared at the door. "You're under arrest for treason to His Majesty," they said. "And your goods are confiscated."

The miller put up his fists and said, "You'll not be eating a mouthful of this good American corn, if I can help it."

When the soldiers heard this, they seized the miller and cursed him for a rebel. Warner twisted free and fought bravely, but they overpowered him.

"We'll drown you in the river, you traitor!" snapped their leader, a big soldier with cruel eyes.

"Go ahead," Warner challenged. "But if you throw me in the river, you British buzzards, the banshee that lives there will haunt you the rest of your lives. Oh, I've seen her in the river mist, under the moon, crying like a lost soul. Sure as the stars are in the sky, she'll get you."

At this, the five other soldiers hesitated. "Let's wait until the commander arrives," one said. "He'll decide for us."

"Yes," his fellows agreed.

But the big soldier cursed and said, "Why wait? We were sent on ahead to make the way safe. We'll get rid of this rebel before he makes any more trouble."

On his orders, the soldiers carried the miller down to the riverbank. They bound his hands behind him and tied heavy stones around his neck and ankles. Then they threw him into the river. As his body sank from sight, an ear-shattering cry rang from bank to bank—the cry of a woman in the agony of death.

The soldiers froze in fear. At first, they saw nothing but evening mist rising over the water. Then the mist took the shape of a woman with flowing hair and a veil over her face. The men paled in horror.

"The banshee," groaned one of the men who stood gaping at the sight. Suddenly the cruel-eyed leader, who had been so eager to drown the miller, turned and fled to the mill. After a moment, the others followed. Behind them, the veiled figure screamed again, then dissolved in the darkening air.

Shortly after nightfall, the commander and the rest of the British troops arrived. While the officers took up quarters in the mill house, the soldiers pitched tents beneath the trees and lit campfires.

A new moon arose, thin and yellow. Far off, a rain crow called for rain. Then, shattering the stillness, came the banshee's bone-chilling cry.

The commander and his officers rushed from the mill house. The soldiers tumbled from their tents—all except the soldier with evil eyes, and his mates who had helped him drown the miller. They sat motionless, with their hands over their ears, trying to stifle the agonizing wail.

The astonished officers on the bank saw a thick cloud of mist above the river slowly take the form of a woman with flowing hair. From beneath the veil that hid her face came the weird cries that echoed down the stream. After a few minutes, the figure began to fade, though her cries lingered a long time.

When the commander questioned his men about the unearthly figure, the guilty men—nearly frightened out of their wits—confessed their crime. The angry commander, for punishment, sentenced them to spend the rest of their enlistments at the mill, grinding grain and listening to the haunting wail.

During the day, the six worked without resting, while

the banshee's cries tormented their sleepless nights. Then, upon a midnight, the banshee appeared in the doorway of the mill—a tall, mist-shrouded figure with flowing hair. She flung back her veil and faced the frightened men. Her fearsome eyes burned into the very souls of all but the cruel-eyed soldier, who buried his face in his hands and hid behind the millstone.

Without taking her fiery, hypnotic eyes off her victims, the banshee began to recede into the night. Like dreamers, the five men followed blindly. Out over the river she floated, and they followed her, pushing through the mud and reeds, until they were caught by the current, which had become unaccountably swift. Without a struggle, they were swallowed by the dark water and never seen again.

After that, the evil-eyed soldier was left alone. He would lock the door of the mill and stuff his ears with bits of sacking, but the mocking cry of the banshee pierced his head and heart. After a time, he went mad. He wandered the riverbank calling, "David Warner! Have pity on me!" But only the wail of the banshee answered him. One day, his body was found floating face upward in the very place in the river where he had drowned the miller.

So the sad tale ended—save for the throbbing cry of the banshee, which can still be heard above the river mists every August, when the rain crow calls for rain beneath a thin, yellow moon.

The Deadly Violin

(Germany—Jewish traditional)

Long ago, in the German city of Worms, Nahum the carpenter was hired to make a coffin. The dead man's family provided the wood, warning Nahum that it should be used only for the casket. But when his work was finished, the carpenter found he had one board left. Never one to waste so much as a scrap, Nahum decided to fashion the leftover wood into a violin.

During the night, however, Nahum had a dream in which the dead man, who had been laid to rest in the coffin, came to him and said, "Cast the remaining wood into the fire; don't turn it to any other purpose."

But when the carpenter woke up, he told himself, "That was merely a dream."

That morning, he began to carve and shape the wood into a violin. He worked slowly to ensure that everything about the instrument would be the best. Since he loved to play the violin, he eagerly imagined the time when he would finally carve the bow and coax the first notes from his handiwork.

Every night the dead man came to him in a dream, telling Nahum, "Cast the wood into the fire." And every morning the carpenter dismissed the warning. He put no value in dreams.

At last the instrument was finished. Joyfully Nahum carved and strung a bow. Lovingly he polished the violin,

198

so that it gleamed in the light of his candles. Since it had grown very late, he decided to wait until the next morning to try out the violin.

Again the dead man came to Nahum's dreams. "Cast the wood into the fire," said the spectral voice. "This is the last time I will warn you."

Awakening the next morning, the carpenter told himself, "That was a good dream, since the ghost has promised not to bother me anymore."

Straightaway, Nahum took down the violin from the shelf and tenderly drew the bow across its strings. As if it were playing itself, the violin poured forth the strains of a haunting melody—a tune the carpenter had never heard before. The bow seemed to glide without his guidance; the violin under his chin trembled like a living creature. The music filled his head with visions of strange landscapes where pale figures wandered.

Nahum began to grow frightened, but he could not keep himself from playing the song to its end. The moment the final haunting note died away, the room grew as dark as if the sun had been blotted out. With a cry, Nahum ran to the window, threw it open, and peered outside. But the darkness was so thick in the street beyond that he could see nothing.

Suddenly a great force—like huge, invisible hands— shoved the carpenter out the window. The terror-stricken man found himself tumbling down. Nahum flung out his arms, but could find nothing to grab hold of. A moment later, he plunged into something soft and wet—like mud.

As he struggled to keep his head above the surface of the ooze, he felt he was being pulled down, as though what he had fallen into was quicksand. The more he resisted, the stronger the downward pull became. Soon he was thrashing about in the blackness, up to his chest in the unseen muck. He cried out again and again for help, but the silence was as absolute as the darkness.

With a violent wrench, the quicksand dragged him under. He felt the thick, moist darkness flood his mouth and throat and lungs.

Then he felt nothing at all.

The next morning, Nahum's son found his father's body lying on the floor of the workshop, the violin still clutched in the stiff fingers of one outstretched hand, the bow locked in his other hand. With a sob, the young man tried to revive his father, but it was no use. In his grief, the lad put the violin up on the shelf and forgot about it.

But that night, the dead man who had warned Nahum came to his son in a dream. The ghostly figure explained all that had happened, and urged the young man to destroy the haunted violin.

The very next day, Nahum's son burned the violin. And as it went up in flames, he heard the anguished voice of his father crying out as if from a great distance. To his dismay, he realized that, somewhere, Nahum's soul was still being punished for his misdeed.

A Night of Terrors

(United States—urban folklore)

"**A**re you sure you'll be all right?" Linda asked the young woman sitting against mounded pillows on the bed.

"I'll be fine," Mary Jo said. "I know you don't want to miss Jack's frat party later." She shifted slightly in the bed. "I am going to be so *glad* to get rid of this flu."

"It still seems like a lousy way to spend Christmas," said Linda. "Everyone else is gone, and now I'm leaving you all alone."

"You'll only be gone a few hours," answered Mary Jo. She dropped her hand beside the bed. From underneath—his favorite hideaway—her dog's muzzle poked out. His pink tongue licked her hand affectionately. "And I've got Jeffy to guard me."

Linda walked to the window. The big house, which the two of them shared with four other college sophomores, was a mile west of the little college town. The nearest house was dark and silent. The Johnsons, retired teachers, had left to visit family in Florida.

"I'll heat up something for dinner," said Linda. "Then I'm going to take a hot bath and get ready for tonight."

"Thanks," Mary Jo said. As she picked up one of the magazines stacked beside her pillow, she lowered her hand again.

Jeffy obligingly licked it. It gave Mary Jo a good feeling to know that the dog would be around when Linda was gone.

Mary Jo fell asleep, but she awoke with a start. Someone was knocking loudly on the front door. It was dark outside. She felt feverish. Groggy, she looked at the clock: 6:53.

Louder knocking. Under the bed, Jeffy growled. More knocking. "Give it a rest!" Mary Jo muttered, but her mouth was dry and her voice was papery. She could barely hear herself.

"All right, already!" yelled Linda from her bedroom across the hall. As she passed Mary Jo's door, she said, "Jack told me he'd come by early because of the snow. But he's an *hour* early!" As the pounding started again, Linda shouted, "Wait a minute! I'm coming down."

She darted back into her room for her coat and fleece-lined gloves. "You *sure* you're gonna be okay?" she asked.

Mary Jo nodded.

Suddenly Jeffy shot out from under the bed and charged downstairs, baying like the hound of the Baskervilles.

"Great!" said Linda. "I finally get a decent date, and you sic your dog on him."

"I'll get Jeffy," said Mary Jo. She started to get up, but her temples and the back of her neck began to throb, and she felt a rush of dizziness and weakness.

"I'll handle Jeffy," said Linda. "You stay put. See you in a couple of hours." She followed the dog downstairs, yelling, "Jeffy! You scare off my date and you're *toast*!"

At the front door, Jeffy was barking so loudly, Mary Jo could no longer hear Linda, who must have opened the door. Mary Jo seemed to hear Jack's deep voice shouting, too. Jeffy went crazy. But the dog had never liked Jack.

Her head aching enough to split, Mary Jo sank back into the pillows. She was sure that Linda would be on her case because of Jeffy. Feeling as rotten as she did, Mary Jo dreaded the idea of a confrontation. The commotion downstairs stopped as though sliced off.

"Thank you all very much," she whispered.

The front door slammed.

"Bye, kids, have fun," she murmured. "I won't wait up."

She started to shiver. Feeling as though it was a monumental effort, she reached out and snapped off the bedside lamp. Then she burrowed as deep into the bedclothes as she could. But she still felt chilled, and more tired than ever.

Vaguely she wondered, Where's Jeffy? She hoped he wasn't making a mess. "I'll sort everything out later," she promised herself as she drifted off to sleep.

In her feverish sleep, Mary Jo sensed, more than heard, Jeffy come into the room. He was panting. She dreaded to think what he'd been up to. Probably running up and down and jumping on the furniture. "Under the bed, Jeffy," she commanded. "Be good, and give me a kiss," she said, reaching down to him.

He obediently licked her hand.

"Good boy," she said as she drifted back to sleep.

The phone on the nightstand woke her.

Jack pounding on the door. Barking Jeffy. Yelling Linda. Ringing phone. To a sick and exhausted Mary Jo, it seemed like a conspiracy to make noise and wake her up. "Go 'way," she ordered the phone as it jangled

again. She hated the sound of the phone's bell in this rented house. She hated whoever was calling. She wanted only silence and sleep. Maybe she should curl up with Jeffy under the bed and wish the whole world away.

The phone continued to ring.

Exasperated, she plucked the receiver from its cradle, dragged it under the covers, and asked, "Who is it?"

"Linda?" a man's voice asked. She knew the voice. Almost.

"I'm Mary Jo. Linda's gone."

"Gone? Gone where?" The voice was upset. "It's Jack. Mary Jo, you sound funny. What's going on?"

"I'm sick. I've got the campus crud," she said. "But Linda went with you—what time is it?"

"After nine," he said. "I hit a patch of black ice and spun into a ditch on my way there. I finally got a tow, but now I can't get there because of the roadblocks."

"What roadblocks? You're not making any sense, Jack!"

"The police have cordoned off the area," Jack said in a rush. "There was a jailbreak early today. Three criminally insane lifers got out. A car they stole was found around here, so the police are combing the area. I can't get through. But where's Linda? Did she get tired of waiting for me and drive herself in?"

Nothing seemed to make sense to Mary Jo. "I heard her go out," she said. "I heard you. I mean, I *thought* I heard you. I'm sure it was a man's voice downstairs. Jeffy was barking a lot."

"Something's wrong," Jack said. The fear in his voice chilled Mary Jo more than the flu. Her teeth began to chatter.

There was a crash from downstairs. Something heavy and metal went over, and there was the sound of shattering glass. She expected Jeffy to go crazy, but she heard him retreat farther under the bed. What awful thing downstairs unnerved him so?

"Mary Jo! Talk to me!" Jack was shouting into phone. "What's going on?"

"There's someone downstairs," she whispered. "Call the police!"

"Can you get out of there?" he asked. "Can you lock yourself in? Those escapees are apparently really wacked out."

"I— *Help me, Jack, please!* I'm scared."

She could hear Jack shouting to someone in the background. She caught the words *police* and *emergency*.

There was another crash downstairs. The noise spilled into the phone from the extension phone below. Someone had pulled or knocked the downstairs receiver off the hook. A torrent of gasping, gurgling sounds came from the earpiece.

Jack heard it, too. "What's that? Who's on the line? Mary Jo, the police are on the way. Get out! Hide! *Now!*" Then his voice was drowned out by a horrible moaning. Mary Jo slammed down the receiver to shut off the ghastly sound. Realizing that she had just cut herself off from Jack, she picked up the phone. It buzzed, and a recorded voice advised her that the receiver was off the hook. Then the phone gave off a series of shrill electronic pulses. She hung up, afraid that the sound would attract the attention of whoever was downstairs.

Dizzy, unsteady, she crossed to the door and peered toward the top of the stairs. She thought she saw a shadow moving. Or was it her fevered imagination? At that moment the power failed and the hall lights went out.

As quietly as possible, Mary Jo closed and locked the

hall door. The door was sturdy, but she doubted it could hold out long against someone trying to break in. She went to the window, but the sheer drop down to the burlap-covered rosebushes made escape impossible. She looked around for something to use to defend herself. Two heavy ceramic bookends to throw would be her first line of defense. She also grabbed a metal letter opener.

The silence was more frightening than any noise. The room had grown freezing. She retreated to the bed, wrapping the blankets around her. Impulsively she dropped her hand down. After a moment, Jeffy licked it. *Jeffy. Her final defense. Or was he too cowed to be any help at all?*

Minutes passed. Then she heard a scratching and gasping out in the hall. Someone was making his painful way toward her closed door. She pressed her hands to her mouth, to bottle up the scream she felt building up inside.

Whoever was out there had reached the door. Nails scratched the lower panels.

In the distance, she heard the wail of police sirens.

More scraping at the door.

She reached for Jeffy, felt her hand licked again.

Then there was banging on the front door; the sound of splintering wood; heavy footsteps on the stairs; shouts in the hallway; Jack's voice. Without thinking, Mary Jo pulled open the door. Linda was huddled on the hall floor, while Jack and several police officers bent over her. She was badly injured, but still alive. "It was Linda!" Mary Jo gasped. "She was hurt, and I wouldn't let her in. I was afraid." She began to cry.

Jack pulled her aside, put his arm around her. Anxious officers questioned her, while others began to search the house and grounds. An ambulance was on the way.

Someone had attacked Linda. He must have fled again into the night. Or he might be hiding.

Linda was taken downstairs, and Mary Jo followed shakily. The house was filled with bobbing flashlight beams. Every corner was searched.

Behind the couch, one of the officers discovered a furry shape matted with blood. They tried to keep her from looking, but Mary Jo looked anyway.

"Jeffy!" she cried. "But it can't be him! He's been up in my room all this time. Under my bed. So scared he couldn't make a sound. He just kept licking my hand."

The officer drew his gun and waved his fellows toward the stairs. "Humans can lick, too," he said.

The Sending

(Iceland)

Long ago, Icelandic folk believed that an evil spirit could be conjured by magic from a human bone. Such a thing was called a *sending*, which means "gift"; but this was an ironic word, since it referred to something evil sent to destroy an enemy. Fortunately, such a sending could be defeated, if one had courage enough. . . .

One such courageous person was Gudrun Grimsdottir, called Gunna for short. A handsome widow, she managed her farm successfully after her husband died. Though she was much sought after by suitors, she lived contentedly in memory of her life with her husband, and had no desire to remarry.

It happened that Sigurdur, a man of evil temper, who was also skilled in the black arts, wanted to wed Gunna. He hoped to add her land to his own. Sigurdur proposed to her many times, and every time she refused him. Finally he warned her that if she turned him down again, things would go badly for her.

Gunna refused his final proposal; but she was prudent, and put herself on her guard.

Her fears proved well founded. One summer afternoon, she was alone in her kitchen, preparing supper for her farmhands. As Gunna worked, she became aware that an unnatural stillness had fallen over the house and over the yard beyond the open window. In spite of the warmth of the day, she suddenly shivered, as if a wintry breeze had invaded the room.

Turning, she saw a shadow, as soft and black as smoke, hovering just outside the door. But there was no one around to cast such a shadow. Scarcely daring to breathe, Gunna peered more closely at the dark shape: a single spot of white glowed at the inky center of what she could now see had the dimensions of a real man.

She backed toward the larder. At the same time, the pitch-black figure glided in through the kitchen door. Then it began drifting toward the larder. She was trapped inside.

Backing more deeply into the storage space, Gunna felt with her hand for the knife she had been using to slice mutton a short time before. Quietly, she let her fingers close around its handle. She knew that creatures of air and darkness have no love for an honest iron blade.

Suddenly, with a movement almost too fast for her eye to follow, the horror flew forward at her. Bravely she struck out with her knife at what she knew was the sending's only vulnerable place—the white spot where a human heart would be.

Gunna shouted as she drove the blade home, and felt it bite into something hard. The knife was wrenched from her hand as the shadowy figure spun back and away.

Then, to her amazement, both her attacker and the knife vanished. Seeing that her way was now unblocked, she ran to the kitchen door and shouted for the farmworkers, who came running. When they heard her story, they began a search of the kitchen floor and the yard outside.

Very soon, one of the men poking through the dust
210

and stone of the yard cried out, and picked something up. He brought it inside and placed it on the table. There the stalwart woman and the other workers saw what the man had found: a splintered human bone, with Gunna's knife stuck through it.

Fearful that the thing might still be dangerous, Gunna sent for a sorcerer from the north. When he came, he pulled the bone free of the blade, all the time chanting as the bone twisted like a living thing in his fingers. Finally he cast it into a fire, from which curling black smoke arose. When he caught some in a glass jar and sealed it, the smoke became a fly that buzzed angrily inside its glass prison. But the magician told Gunna that the insect was actually a demon. "You must return this to its sender," he said, "or more evil will befall you." Then he told her what she had to do.

The next morning, Gunna put the jar in a beautiful box of beaten gold. She put on her finest gown, and saddled her best horse. Then she set out for her wicked neighbor's farm.

Sigurdur's surprise at seeing her alive turned to delight when Gunna said, "I have reconsidered your offer of marriage. If you will have me, I will be your wife. And the gift I have brought you will be a token of our betrothal."

So saying, she produced the pretty gold box and lifted the lid. Greedy Sigurdur, eager to see what treasure it held, drew close. Quickly Gunna pulled out the jar and threw it, so that it broke on the stone floor at the man's feet.

Thick smoke boiled up and poured into Sigurdur's ears and nose and mouth. His body began to swell; his face grew brutish; his skin turned bluish black. He became a mountain troll, bellowing and grabbing clumsily

211

at her. But agile Gunna eluded his grasp. With a triumphant cry, she fled the house into the daylight, for trolls cannot abide the sun's rays. As she rode away, she heard the sun-cursed creature roaring angrily, helplessly after her.

The Hand of Fate

(British Isles—Wales)

Walter Vaughan was lord of Dunraven Castle, which brooded over a dangerous stretch of Welsh coast. Many ships had been wrecked on the rocks below its battlements. The castle itself had fallen into disrepair, for Vaughan was a spendthrift who had wasted his inheritance. A widower with no friends, he had only one joy in life: his son, Andrew.

But when Andrew grew older, he decided to seek his fortune in foreign lands, since the family money was gone. His father begged him to stay; when Andrew would not be persuaded, Lord Dunraven placed his own gold signet ring on the young man's finger. "Promise me that you will return this to me in your own good time," he said.

"I promise," said Andrew. Then he set out for the nearest port to become a sailor on a merchant ship.

Shortly after father and son had separated, a cargo ship was wrecked near the castle. Though all hands drowned in the churning waves, several chests and barrels filled with valuable goods washed ashore. Tradition said that such property "cast up by the sea" belonged to the lord of the manor. In this way, fate gave Vaughan unexpected riches, but also snatched away his last shreds of decency.

213

Still grieved by the absence of his son, and by the ruin he had brought upon his estate, Vaughan decided to rebuild his failed fortunes by luring other ships to disaster on Dunraven's rocky shore. Then he could become wealthier than ever, restore the Dunraven name, and call his son home.

To help with this scheme, Vaughan sought the help of a disreputable man known as Matt-of-the-Iron-Hand. This wretch had captained a pirate ship many years before. On one occasion, his vessel had been seized by the order of Vaughan, then a magistrate. A desperate struggle had erupted in which Captain Matt had lost one hand, later replaced by an iron hook. From that day, the evil ex-captain became a wrecker, who used a variety of tricks to lure ships onto the rocks so that they could be plundered.

Captain Matt had never forgiven Lord Dunraven, whom he blamed for his ruin. But drawn into Vaughan's scheme, he put aside his hatred for a time. Though Vaughan and this ruffian were never seen together in daylight, they were constant companions by night. Vaughan spent the nights in a cave below his castle, from which he had a clear view of the western ocean. When he spotted the lights of a cargo ship, he signaled to Matt-of-the-Iron-Hand, who lit a series of lanterns. Thinking these were harbor lights, the crew of the unlucky ship would steer coastward. Rocks and treacherous waves soon caused the vessel to founder and break apart. Whatever salvage came their way, the two criminals divided. If any crewmen or passengers survived, they were quickly done away with by the ex-pirate.

As ill-gotten gain filled his coffers, and dreams of his son's return filled his head, Vaughan grew more uneasy in his dealings with Matt-of-the-Iron-Hand. But his attempts to part company with the ex-captain were met by sneers and threats.

Vaughan increasingly feared discovery by the magistrates, and he suffered from the taunts of Matt-of-the-Iron-Hand, whose contempt grew daily. The strain aged Vaughan. He spent every day watching the horizon for ships—not to wreck them, but in the hope that one would carry his son, Andrew, home. In the old man's mind, all would come right when he and his son clasped hands again.

One stormy evening, he saw a ship making its way slowly up the channel, as though her crew were on the lookout for some inlet where temporary shelter could be had. But the gloom of the worsening storm soon hid the vessel from sight.

Vaughan felt unexplainably anxious about the ship; more than ever, he was aware of Matt-of-the-Iron-Hand's hatred, as the wrecker busied himself in the night.

The wind rose, accompanied by drizzling rain. Vaughan's worry grew as the false lights of the ex-pirate threw a lurid glow across the breakers. Soon Vaughan heard, above the howling wind, the crash of a ship breaking up on the rocks, and desperate cries for help. Then there was silence.

Some thirty minutes later, Matt-of-the-Iron-Hand entered the cave and told Vaughan that all but one member of the ship's crew had drowned. The sole survivor, Matt said, turned out to be the captain, who had said that he was a Welshman and a native of Dunraven.

"Did he tell you his name?" asked Vaughan.

A devilish laugh was the only answer as the wrecker thrust a death-cold hand into Vaughan's own. Vaughan recoiled in horror as the torchlight lit up the familiar gold signet ring on the dead finger, and the father knew he clasped the hand of his only son, Andrew.

The murderer slipped away into the night, laughing like a madman. But the sound was drowned by the howls of horror and loss torn from the throat of Vaughan. Dropping to his knees, the distraught father clutched the dreadful object to his chest, aghast at what his crimes had cost his son and himself.

Old Raw Head

(United States—the South)

There was a conjure man down South named High Walker. He could make the bones and skulls in a graveyard rise up, shake themselves, dance around, and lie down again. He lived by himself in the woods. His only companion was a wild razorback hog, which would come down out of the hills and root through his leavings. Sometimes High Walker swept spilled goofer dust and herbs and conjure powder onto the trash heap, and the hog ate them. Gradually, that hog got to where he could walk on two legs and talk like a man. He grew fat, too; that was his undoing.

Turned out there was a hunter nearby. When he saw the size of the hog's hoofprint, his mouth began to water at the thought of all that pork roaming the woods. So he tracked the big old razorback and surprised the hog in a forest clearing as it was on its way to the conjure man's cabin.

The hunter was so excited to have caught up with the hog, his first shot went wild.

The hog reared up on its hind legs, looked across the clearing, and said, "What do you want?"

"I want to eat the jowl and ham and chop of you," said the man. He fired again, and that was the end of the razorback. The hunter stripped all the meat off the carcass, and left only the raw head and bloody bones scattered on the forest floor.

Late in the day, the conjure man, wondering what had become of the hog, stumbled across the skinned head and peeled bones. Right away he called, "Bloody Bones, get up, shake yourselves."

So the ghastly remains pulled themselves together, stood up, and rattled themselves. Then Raw Head and Bloody Bones walked into the woods.

As he stalked along, he recollected some of the magic he had digested from the conjure man's trash pile. He conjured himself as tall as, or taller, than a pine tree. He saw an owl and conjured himself eyes as big or bigger. He saw a mountain lion and conjured himself fangs as sharp or sharper. When he saw a bear, he conjured himself claws as fierce or fiercer. When he spotted a raccoon's tail, he conjured himself a tail as bushy or bushier.

Through the moonlight, Raw Head and Bloody Bones stalked until he stopped outside the hunter's cabin.

There he took hold of the chimney and rattled it.

When the sleeping hunter woke up and peeked out the window, he exclaimed, "What do you need such big eyes for?"

"To see your grave," Raw Head and Bloody Bones answered.

"What do you need such a big old tail for?"

"To sweep your grave."

"Why do you need such long, fierce claws?"

"To catch you and take you deep in the woods."

"And what do you want with such sharp teeth?"

"To eat you, jowl and ham and chop."

The hunter slammed and barred the door, and closed

the window shutters, but none of this did a lick of good. Raw Head and Bloody Bones just lifted up the roof, snatched the hunter out from under the bed, and stalked off with him into the night.

Nothing more was seen of the hunter. But Raw Head and Bloody Bones is still around. Sometimes, on a moon-shiny night, people around those parts hear strange *clickity-clackity, rattlely-clattery* sounds, deep in the piney woods. This means Old Raw Head and Bloody Bones is dancing and stalking about. Then, good Christian folk had best say their prayers, and pull the bedclothes up, and hope that morning comes real soon.

Notes on Sources

THE MOUSE TOWER.   Adapted from accounts in *Curious Myths of the Middle Ages* by Reverend Sabine Baring-Gould (London: Rivingtons, 1866), and an account in *The German Legends of the Brothers Grimm, Volume I,* edited and translated by Donald Ward (Philadelphia, Penn.: Institute for the Study of Human Issues Incorporated, 1981). The Grimms' work was originally published in 1816. See also *The Finest Legends of the Rhine* by William Ruland (Bonn, Germany: Stollfuss Verlag, 1969).

    Baring-Gould argues that the real-life Bishop Hatto was not "hard-hearted and wicked" and that "the [mouse] tower was erected as a station for collecting tolls on vessels passing up and down the river." Maria Leach, editor of *Funk & Wagnalls Standard Dictionary of Folklore, Mythology, and Legend,* notes that stories of a miser devoured by mice or rats in a tower are widespread throughout Germany, Austria, Switzerland, Poland, and Scandinavia.

THE DEVIL AND TOM WALKER.   This account was first published in Washington Irving, *Tales of a Traveller* (New York: 1825; reprinted in *The Works of Washington Irving, Volume I,* New York: P.F. Collier, n.d.). Folklorist Richard M. Dorson, in his *Jonathan Draws the Long Bow: New England Popular Tales and Legends* (Cambridge, Mass.: Harvard University Press, 1946), comments that it is a literary tale that has evolved into regional folklore, noting that the story was included in Charles M. Skinner's *Myths and Legends of Our Own Land, Volume I* (Philadelphia: J.B. Lippincott Company, 1896).

THE GREEDY DAUGHTER.   Adapted from the story of the same title originally published in R.H. Busk, *The Folk-Lore of Rome* (n.d.), reprinted in *Folk Tales of All Nations,* edited by F.H. Lee (New York: Tudor Publishing Company, 1930). I also consulted the more extended and earthier version titled "Uncle Wolf" in *Italian Folktales,* selected and retold by Italo Calvino, published in Italy in 1956; English translation by George Martin (New York: Harcourt Brace Jovanovich, 1980); available in paperback in *The Pantheon Fairy Tale and Folklore Library* (New York: Random House, 1981).

THE PIRATE. Adapted from Richard H. Dana's eighteenth-century poem "The Buccaneer," reprinted with commentary in Samuel Adams Drake, *A Book of New England Legends and Folk Lore: In Prose and Poetry* (first edition, 1884; revised, 1906; reprinted, Boston: Charles E. Tuttle, 1971). I have also consulted the prose version by Charles M. Skinner in his *Myths and Legends of Our Own Land* (Philadelphia: J.B. Lippincott Company, 1896). These accounts are loosely based on the actual burning of the ship *Palantine* in the winter of 1750-51, which gave rise to many tales about a blazing ghostly vessel.

THE GOLDEN ARM. Adapted and expanded from Joseph Jacobs, *English Fairy Tales* (London, 1890), this tale is akin to such formula stories as the English "Teeny Tiny," in which a teeny-tiny woman takes a teeny-tiny bone from a churchyard to make some teeny-tiny soup, and "Tailypo," from the American South, retold in the first volume of *Short & Shivery* (New York: Bantam Doubleday Dell, 1986).

Folklorist Maria Leach comments in her *The Thing at the Foot of the Bed: And Other Scary Tales* (Cleveland, Ohio: William Collins & World Publishing Company, 1959; reprinted by New York: Bantam Doubleday Dell, 1977), "This is one of the most famous scary stories told. It is said to have been told around every Boy and Girl Scout campfire ever kindled . . . the story Mark Twain used to tell to scare whole audiences."

THE SERPENT WOMAN. This tale has been condensed and rewritten from the story of the same title originally published in Mrs. Middlemore, *Spanish Legendary Tales* (n.d.), reprinted in *Folk Tales of All Nations* edited by F.H. Lee (New York: Tudor Publishing Company, 1930). The story uses the familiar element of the witch transformed into another form (black cat, raven, serpent) and discovered when a wound inflicted on the animal is revealed in its human form. For a parallel, one might look at "The Witch Cat" in my first *Short & Shivery* collection.

There is also an echo of the swan-maiden or seal-maiden motif in which magical beings put aside a coat of feathers of a fishskin to become beautiful, seemingly human women.

LOFT THE ENCHANTER. Adapted from accounts in *Ghosts, Witchcraft, and the Other World: Icelandic Folktales I,* translated by Alan Boucher (Reykjavik, Iceland: Iceland Review Library, 1977) and *Legends of Icelandic Magicians,* translated by Jacqueline Simpson (Cambridge, England: D.S. Brewer, Ltd.; Totowa, N.J.: Rowan and Littlefield, 1975). Additional background details are from *Nagel's*

Encyclopedia-Guide: Iceland, Third Edition, Completely Revised (Geneva, Paris, Munich: Nagel Publishers, 1984) and *A Family in Iceland: Families Around the World Series* (New York: The Bookwright Press, 1985).

THE ACCURSED HOUSE. Adapted and expanded from an account in Charles M. Skinner, *Myths & Legends of Our Own Land: Volume II* (Philadelphia: J.B. Lippincott Company, 1896). This story picks up the classic folkloric theme of the ghost who guards a hidden treasure.

ESCAPE UP THE TREE. I based this story on a Nigerian version of a well-known African tale because of the unique form the pursuing creature takes. I have added details from Caribbean versions—clearly from African roots—from the islands of Trinidad, Martinique, Dominica, Guadeloupe, Les Saintes, and Haiti. In these stories, a witch, a female demon, or the devil himself forces a boy/young man to escape up the tree. The tale has similarities to "Brother and Sister" in the first *Short & Shivery* collection. In the United States, a variant story is widely known as "Wiley and the Hairy Man." Here a young boy is eventually trapped by the hairy man or the devil, and is rescued by his three (or four) dogs.

For the originals, see "The Hunter and the Witch" in *Nigerian Folk Tales*, as told by Olawale Idewu and Omotayo Adu (New Brunswick, N.J.: Rutgers University Press, 1961). See also variants grouped under the heading "Escape Up the Tree" in *Folk-Lore of the Antilles, French and English, Part III*, by Elsie Clews Parsons (first published by the American Folk-Lore Society in 1943; reprinted, New York: Kraus Reprint Company, 1969). Maria Leach discusses the tale in *God Had a Dog: Folklore of the Dog* (New Brunswick, N.J.: Rutgers University Press, 1961).

THE HEADREST. Retold from Annie Ker's *Papuan Fairy Tales* (c.1912), a collection of folktales from the northeastern coast of New Guinea, reprinted in F.H. Lee, *Folk Tales of All Nations* (New York: Tudor Publishing Company, 1930). Mrs. Ker lived at a mission compound in New Guinea in 1910.

THE THING IN THE WOODS. Adapted from an account in *Gumbo Ya-Ya: A Collection of Louisiana Folk Tales* by Lyle Saxon, Robert Tallant, and Edward Dryer (first published in 1945 by Louisiana Writers Project Publications; reprinted, New York: Bonanza Books, n.d.). Details of Cajun life and language came from William Faulkner Rushton, *The Cajuns: From Acadia to Louisiana* (New York: Farrar, Straus & Giroux, 1970), and other sources.

The Cajuns live mainly in rural southern Louisiana, are largely Roman Catholic, and are the largest French-speaking group in the United States. "Cajun" comes from "Acadian," referring to the part of Canada to which their ancestors came from France. Those early French settlers immigrated to Louisiana after their farms were seized and burned by the English governor of Nova Scotia in 1755. Henry Wadsworth Longfellow tells the story of their exile in his poem *Evangeline*.

KING OF THE CATS. Adapted from Joseph Jacobs's classic *More English Fairy Tales* (London, 1894). Jacobs's version, which is widely anthologized, was put together by that author from several earlier narratives. He cites five variants of the legend, commenting, "An interesting example of the spread and development of a single anecdote throughout England . . . a tale which is, in its way, as weird and fantastic as E[dgar] A[llan] Poe."

THE DEAD MOTHER. Retold from *Russian Folk Tales* by William R. Shedden-Ralston (London, 1873); reprinted in Bernhardt J. Hurwood, *Passport to the Supernatural: An Occult Compendium from All Ages and Many Lands* (New York: Taplinger Publishing Company, 1972).

KNOCK . . . KNOCK . . . KNOCK . . . A retelling of one of the most popular examples of urban folklore. In *The Vanishing Hitchhiker: American Urban Legends & Their Meanings* (New York: W.W. Norton & Company, 1981), Jan Harold Brunvand offers an extended discussion of this "well-known urban legend that folklorists have named 'The Boyfriend's Death' . . . a story that has traveled rapidly to reach nationwide oral circulation." In *Folklore of Canada* (Canada: McClelland and Stewart, 1976), Edith Fowke refers to "The Boyfriend's Death" as being "widely known today . . . Such legends are particularly rife among teen-agers, who sometimes call them 'scary stories.' These tales, which are always sworn to be true, are told at social get-togethers such as pajama parties, nights at summer camps, canoe trips, or camp reunions."

TWICE SURPRISED. This is one of the most widely repeated ghost stories in Japan. It is known variously under such titles as "Surprised Twice," "The Terrible Face," "The Ghost Covered with Eyes," "The Face That Grew Long," "The Eyeless Demon in Monjuroku," and "Was It This Kind of Face?"
I have based this retelling on a version in *Ancient Tales in Modern*

Japan: An Anthology of Japanese Folk Tales, selected and translated by Fanny Hagin Mayer (Bloomington: Indiana University Press, copublished with *Asian Folklore Studies*, 1984), and on a study of the story and its variants found in *The Yanagita Kunio guide to the Japanese Folk Tale* by Yanagita Kunio, translated and edited by Fanny Hagin Mayer (Bloomington: Indiana University Press, copublished with *Asian Folklore Studies*, 1986). The latter volume is a translation of *Nihon Mukashibanashi Meii*, originally published in Tokyo in 1948.

APPOINTMENT IN SAMARRA. One of the world's best-known tales has been retold in many versions over the years, but it never loses its ironic impact. The Middle Eastern story underscores the folly of trying to escape one's destiny. The Koran, the scripture of the Islamic faith, teaches that Allah has created both life and death, that the time of death has been "written" (predestined) for all people, and that death will reach a person anywhere, so flight is useless. One variant I consulted was that in *The Enchanted World: Ghosts* by the Editors of Time-Life Books (Alexandria, Virginia: Time-Life Books, Inc., 1984). Death is widely personified as a woman. (See "Sister Death and the Healer," in *Short & Shivery*, as an example from Mexico and Spain.)

DEER WOMAN. I have retold this Native American story from a version in *American Indian Mythology* by Alice Marriott and Carol K. Rachlin (New York: Thomas Y. Crowell Company, Inc., 1968), retold in abbreviated form in *American Folklore and Legend* by the Editors of Reader's Digest General Books (Pleasantville, New York: The Reader's Digest Association, Inc., 1978). "The Ponca were primarily farmers but engaged in seasonal buffalo hunts. They are part of the Siouan linguistic family, and their name has been interpreted by some authorities as 'That Which Is Sacred.'"–*Plains Indians: Dog Soldiers, Bear Men, and Buffalo Women*, written and illustrated by Thomas E. Mails (New York: Prentice-Hall, Inc., 1973; reprint, New York: Promontory Press, 1993). I incorporated details from such books as *Funk & Wagnalls Standard Dictionary of Folklore, Mythology, and Legend: An Unabridged Edition of the Original Work with a Key to Place Names, Cultures, and People*, edited by Maria Leach (New York: Harper & Row Publishers, Inc., 1949, 1950, 1972; paperback reprint, Harper San Francisco, 1982), *Indians on Horseback* by Alice Marriott (New York: Thomas Y. Crowell Co., 1948), and *Mystic Warriors of the Plains: The Culture, Arts, Crafts, and Religion of the Plains Indians*, written and illustrated by Thomas E. Mails (New York: Mallard Press/BBD Promotional Books, 1991; reprint of a book originally published in 1972).

THE MAGGOT. I have retold this story from a brief account in "A Quartet of Strange Things," by Bernhardt J. Hurwood, included in *Ghosts: A Treasury of Chilling Tales Old & New,* selected by Marvin Kaye with Saralee Kaye (New York: Doubleday and Company, 1981). Hurwood claims the story is a true one. He told the story rather differently as "The Monstrous Maggot of Death" in *Monsters and Nightmares* (New York: Bellamont Books, 1967). "The Flyin' Childer" and Sam'l's Ghost" in *Legends of the Lincolnshire Cars* (1891) by M.C. Balfour show the dead as huge worms. The concept of the maggot may derive from the ancient Roman belief in an evil ghost called a larva, which frightened people and worked ill against them. It also seems connected with the notion of ectoplasm, a ghostly, milky-white substance supposedly produced at séances, which can shape itself into spirit limbs, faces, or bodies.

WITCH WOMAN. A retelling of one of the better-known African American folktales. Among the variants consulted were "Skin Don't You Know Me?" in *American Negro Folktales,* collected by Richard M. Dorson (Bloomington: Indiana University Press, 1956, 1967; paperback reprint, New York: Fawcett World Library, 1970); "De Wich-'ooman an' de Spinnin'-Wheel" by Mrs. M.E.M. Davis (*The Journal of American Folk-Lore,* Vol. 18, July-September, 1905), reprinted in *A Treasury of American Folklore,* edited by B.A. Botkin New York: Crown Publishers, 1944), and "De Witch Woman" in *The LIFE Treasury of American Folklore* by the Editors of Life (New York: Time Incorporated, 1961). In the American South and the West Indies, such creatures as vampires, loogaroos (from *loup-garous* or werewolves), or witches could be destroyed if their hidden skin could be found and salt and pepper poured into it or pounded in with a mortar. The creature would then be unable to resume its human shape and would perish miserably in the sunlight.

THE BERBALANGS. Retold from "Cagayan Sulu, Its Customs, Legends, and Superstitions" by Ethelbert Skertchley, published in *Journal of the Asiatic Society of Bengal,* Vol. 45, Part 3, Anthropology and Cognate Subjects (Calcutta: Asiatic Society/Baptist Mission Press, 1896); the substance of the article has been reprinted in full, along with extensive commentary, in "The Berbalangs of Cagayan Sulu," a chapter of *Oddities: A Book of Unexplained Facts* by Rupert T. Gould (originally published in London: 1928; revised edition, London: 1944; reprint, New York: Bell Publishing Co., 1965). The Filipino *berbalangs* are part of the nightmarish Asian troop of hunting heads that includes the *kephn* of Burma, a demon in the form of a wizard's head with its stomach attached, which devours souls; the vampiric Malay *penaggalan*, a head that glides along with its dangling intestines gleaming "like fireflies;" and the Japanese goblins in "Rokuro-Kubi," retold in the present volume. Tiny Cagayan Sulu Island sits in the Sulu Sea, which is bordered by the Philippine Islands and Malaysia.

THE DANCING DEAD OF SHARK ISLAND. Adapted from an account in *Ancient Legends of Ireland*, compiled by Sheila Anne Barry (New York: Sterling Publishing Co., Inc., 1996). The material comes from *Ancient Legends, Mystic Charms, & Superstitions of Ireland and Ancient Cures, Charms, and Usages of Ireland*, both by Lady Wilde (1826-1896). The connection of the ghosts with fairies is here hinted at by the dead dancing on a hillside (fairies reportedly lived in hills or mounds) to elfin music. Fairies were often discovered dancing in fairy rings; it was dangerous for a mortal to join in such a dance. A "fairy stroke," a harmful spell cast by a fairy, was believed to cause illness or death in victims. Some thought fairies were ghosts or dispossessed spirits that were lost between heaven and hell.

"THAT I SEE, BUT THIS I SEW." Retold and expanded from a brief account in *The Highlands and Their Legends* by Otta F. Swire (Edinburgh and London: Oliver & Boyd, 1963). Swire comments that there is, indeed, the ruin of an old church near the Scottish village of Beauly (originally named Beaulieu, French for "beautiful place"), identified as the setting for the story of this brave little tailor. Swire also notes that the tailor's reply, "That I see, but this I sew," became a saying used by a person who refused to turn aside from what he or she had set out to do. Another local saying was "The great grizzled one catch you," meaning the Devil, whom it was unlucky to name.

LA GUIABLESSE. Adapted from a narrative included in *Two Years in the French West Indies* by Lafcadio Hearn (New York and London: Harper & Brothers Publishers, 1890). The setting is the Caribbean island of Martinique, where the language spoken is French Creole. In the island language, "Manzell" is a form of "Mademoiselle" (Miss); "Missie" is a form of "Monsieur" (Sir); and "La Guiablesse" is a feminine form indicating a female goblin. This gobliness is unusual in that she haunts the day and vanishes with the sunset. Usually such nightmare beings confine their activities to the hours of darkness.

THE BLOOD-DRAWING GHOST. Retold from the account in *Irish Fairy Tales* by Jeremiah Curtin, first published in the 1890s (reprint

New York: Dorset Press, 1992). Revenants, the returned dead, are familiar figures in Irish tales. A somewhat similar tale, "Teg O'Kane and the Corpse," in *Irish Tales of Terror*, 1971; reprint, New York: Bonanza Books, 1988), tells of a corpse-ridden young man who spends a terrifying night trying to find a suitable grave for his ghastly "passenger." A version of "The Blood Drawing Ghost" virtually identical to the Irish original, but set in the American Southwest, is entitled "Mary Calhoun," after the heroine, who is forced to carry "something very, very old and dead [that] sat on her shoulders," and who saves the handsome son of the third household as in the original. See *Ghost Stories of the American Southwest* by Richard Alan Young and Judy Dockrey Young (originally published by Little Rock: August House, 1991; reprinted with *Ghost Stories from the American South* in a combined edition entitled *Ghastly Ghost Stories*, New Jersey: Wing Books, 1993).

GUESTS FROM GIBBET ISLAND. Abridged and edited from the story by Washington Irving that first appeared in *Wolfert's Roost* (1855), a collection of tales and sketches. The original text can be found in The *Complete Tales of Washington Irving*, edited with an introduction by Charles Neider (New York: Doubleday & Company, Inc., 1975). A brief account, based on Irving's original, is entitled "The Party from Gibbet Island" in *Myths and Legends of Our Own Land* by Charles M. Skinner (New York: J.B. Lippincott Company, 1896, 1924). As he did with other tales, such as "Rip Van Winkle," Irving transplanted a European folktale to American soil and greatly expanded the original, a tale titled "Guests from the Gallows" collected by the Brothers Grimm. See *The German Legends of the Brothers Grimm—Volume I*, edited and translated by Donald Ward (Philadelphia: Institute for the Study of Human Issues, Inc., 1981).

THE HAUNTED HOUSE. Retold and expanded from a brief account in *The Golden Mountain: Chinese Tales Told in California*, collected by Jon Lee, edited by Paul Radin (Taipei, Taiwan: Caves Books, Ltd., n.d.), with background details from *Chinese Houses and Gardens* by Henry Inn and Shao Chang Lee (New York: Hastings House, Publishers, 1940; reprint, New York: Bonanza Books, 1950).

"NEVER FAR FROM YOU." This is a reworking of a story widely known in Britain, where the events are variously set in Yorkshire, Hampshire, or Oxfordshire. Its popularity was helped by a ballad, "The Mistletoe Bough" by Thomas Haynes Bayley, which musically recounts the tragic story. The song was very popular in the

Victorian and Edwardian eras. In the United States, where many versions are known, the story has been spread orally, and the bride sometimes becomes a princess. Original tellings can be found as "The Lost Bride," in *A Dictionary of British Folk-Tales in the English Language–Part B, Folk Legends* by Katharine M. Briggs (New York and London: Routledge & Kegan Paul, 1970; paperback reprint, 1991), and in *The Folktales of England*, edited by Katherine M. Briggs and Ruth L. Tongue (Chicago: The University of Chicago Press, 1965).

THE ROSE ELF. This is a slightly altered and shortened version of Hans Christian Andersen's tale. Andersen apparently based his telling on Giovanni Boccaccio's fourteenth-century collection of tales, *The Decameron* (Fourth Day/Fifth Story). That tale tells of Elisabetta, whose brothers kill her lover, Lorenzo, and it also inspired the poem "Isabella, or the Pot of Basil" (1820) by John Keats. In turning the gloomy material into a fairy tale, Andersen incorporated the rose elf, including fairy lore popular in his day, which envisioned elves as tiny, winged creatures, often associated with flowers. In fact, the fairy-folk of the oldest folktales were magical beings as tall as humans, who lived in green hills or mounds and had powers they often used to trick or trap humans. Andersen's tale is available in countless collections of his work. I consulted the new translation of *The Decameron* by Mark Musa and Peter Bondanella (New York: The New American Library/Penguin Books USA, 1982). The Keats poem is widely anthologized.

THE WIND RIDER. Adapted from "The Wind Rider" in *Folklore and Legend: Russian and Polish* by "C.J." (published in 1891). The original story has been reprinted in *Lovers, Mates, and Strange Bedfellows: Old-World Folktales* by James R. Foster (New York: Harper & Brothers, 1960). Witches, it was believed, had great power over winds and could call them up by combing out their hair. Mermaids often had the same power. Foster notes that the story is similar to an Italian tale in which Judas is punished by having his soul endlessly blown around the world, so that each day it must pass over the tree on which his body is hanging, being torn apart by dogs and birds of prey.

THE SKULL THAT SPOKE. I have composited this version of a well-known tale from Nigerian sources, but it is also known in the American South. For a full study of this tale as well as variants from Nigeria, Ghana, Senegal, Mali, Togo, Zaire, Malawi, Brazil, Haiti, and the United States, see the chapter "The Talking Skull Refuses to Talk" in *African Folktales in the New World* by William Bascom

(Bloomington and Indianapolis, Indiana: Indiana University Press, 1992). I also consulted such variants as "Talking Bone" in *Universal Myths: Heroes, Gods, Tricksters, and Others* by Alexander Eliot (originally published as *Myths*, London: McGraw-Hill Book CO., Ltd., 1976, paperback reprint, New York: Penguin Books USA, 1990), and "Musakalala, the Talking Skull" from *Congo Fireside Tales* by Phyllis Savory (New York: Hastings House Publishers, Inc., 1962).

THE MONSTER OF BAYLOCK. Adapted from an account by E.M. Stephens, first published in the *Daily News and Westminster Gazette* (n.d.), and reprinted in full in *Folk Tales of All Nations*, edited by F.H. Lee (New York: Coward-McCann, Inc., 1930; reprint, New York: Tudor Publishing Company; 1946; revised edition published as *Classic Folk Tales from Around the World*, with a new introduction, but omitting all source notes, London: Bracken Books, 1994).

THE NEW MOTHER. This story is based on "The Pear-Drum," published by J.Y. Bell in *Folk-Lore: A Quarterly Review of Myth, Tradition, Institution and Customs*, Vol. 46 (London: Folk-Lore Society, 1955), and reprinted in *A Dictionary of British Folk-Tales in the English Language–Part A, Folk Narratives* by Katherine M. Briggs (New York and London: Routledge & Kegan Paul, 1970; paperback reprint, 1991). In the original, the temptress is a gypsy girl. Briggs comments, "This is a family story, and was probably a cautionary tale invented by the first teller in the family. The mother with glass eyes and wooden tail is an unusual invention, but there is an authentic thrill about her." For this telling, I also consulted a much longer version in *Anyhow Stories, Moral and Otherwise* by Lucy Lane Clifford (London: 1882), reprinted in *The Oxford Book of Modern Fairy Tales*, edited by Alison Lurie (Oxford and New York: Oxford University Press, 1993). Discussing the story in The *Penguin Book of English Folktales* (New York: Penguin Books USA, Inc., 1992), editor Neil Philip comments, "The historian of children's literature, F.J. Harvey Darton, was haunted by the figure of the new mother, recording in his *Children's Books in England* that, 'Getting on for fifty years after I met her first, I still cannot rid my mind of that fearful creation.'"

ROKURO-KUBI. Japanese folktales and legends feature some of the ghastliest ghosts and most monstrous monsters in world folklore. I have returned to these traditional sources again and again for delectable shivers. The Rokuro-Kubi, goblins of the dark, are first cousins to the Filipino *berbalangs*, also featured in this collection. For this retelling, I consulted the versions in *Kwaidan: Stories and Studies of Strange Things* by Lafcadio Hearn (first published in 1904; reprinted,

Rutland, Vermont, and Tokyo, Japan: The Charles E. Tuttle Company, Inc., 1971) and "The Goblins' Guest" in *The Enchanted World: Tales of Terror* by the Editors of Time-Life Books.

DICEY AND ORPUS. This is a considerably expanded version of a folktale originally collected in *The Book of Romance*, edited by Andrew Lang (New York: Longmans, Green and Company, 1902; story reprinted in *A Harvest of World Folk Tales*, edited by Milton Rugoff, New York: The Viking Press, 1940; paperback reprint, 1968). This is an African American retelling of the Greek Myth of Orpheus, who played a wondrous lyre, a gift of the god Apollo, so entrancingly that all nature danced to the music. He married Eurydice, who died after being bitten by a snake. Orpheus followed her to the underworld, where his music charmed Hades, the ruler of the dead. Releasing Eurydice, Hades warned Orpheus that if he looked back at his wife before she was safely in sunlight, she would be lost forever. Stepping into the sunshine, Orpheus looked back, and Eurydice, still in shadow, was lost forever. The Greek original is told in full in *A Harvest of World Folk Tales.* The Land of the Golden Slipper was heaven: African American lore held that those who went to heaven wore golden slippers. Here heaven is underground in keeping with the Orpheus story.

CHIPS. Adapted from "Chips and the Devil" in chapter XV, "Nurse's Stories," *The Uncommercial Traveller* (London: 1860) by Charles Dickens, who heard the tale in childhood from a nursemaid, Mary Weller. Katherine M. Briggs includes the story in her monumental *A Dictionary of British Folk-Tales in the English Language: Part A—Folk Narratives* (New York and London: Routledge & Kegan Paul, 1970; paperback reprint, 1991). She points out that the story includes many familiar folktale elements, including the Devil with saucer eyes, the Devil taking the form of a mouse, a rat that speaks, and a ship that sinks because the Devil is aboard. The tale, along with a discussion of Mary Weller's influence on Dickens's writing, can be found in *The Penguin Book of English Folktales*, edited by Neil Philip (New York: Penguin Books USA, Inc., 1992).

THE SKELETON'S REVENGE. Composited from two variants, "Legend of the Puente del Clerigo (Clergyman's Bridge)" in *Legends of the City of Mexico* by Thomas A. Janvier (New York: Harper & Brothers, 1910), and "The Avenging Skeleton" in *Of the Night Wind's Telling: Legends from the Valley of Mexico* by E. Adams Davis (Norman, Oklahoma: University of Oklahoma Press, 1946, reprinted 1976). The skeleton returning from the beyond for vengeance is a worldwide story pattern. Examples include Japan's "The Dancing Skeleton" in *Short & Shivery* and "Guests from Gibbet Island" in the present volume—a story known in both the United States and Germany.

LULLABY. The original was included in the famous collection *Lord Halifax's Ghost Book* (Geoffrey Bles, Ltd., 1936). Lord Halifax insisted the story was true, and that he had heard it from the nephew of the man who actually had the experience. For this retelling, I also consulted the adaptation "Lullaby for the Dead" by Michael and Mollie Hardwick in *50 Great Horror Stories*, edited by John Canning (New York: Bell Publishing Co., 1971; reprint, London: Longmeadow Press, 1985), and a shortened version, "The Ghostly Passenger," in *The Encyclopedia of Ghosts* by Daniel Cohen (New York: Dodd, Mead & Company, Inc., 1984).

DEATH AND THE TWO FRIENDS. Retold from "Death and the Two Bachelors" in *Doctor to the Dead: Grotesque Legends and Folk Tales of Old Charleston* by John Bennett (New York and Toronto: Rinehart & Company, Inc., 1943, 1946). For nearly fifty years before the publication of *Doctor to the Dead*, Bennett had been collecting the folklore of one of South Carolina's most picturesque and historically important cities.

FOREST GHOSTS. Adapted from a long historical account, "The Antlered Master of Château Bois Chasse," in *Gallery of Ghosts* by James Reynolds (New York: The Creative Press, 1949; paperback reprint, New York: Paperback Library, 1970). Reynolds traces the story to events that happened during the reign of King Henri IV (1553-1610), at a place called Château Rochetonnerre. The Green Woman is one of the forest elves called *dames vertes* (green ladies), who were spirits of forest and field. Though the smells of earth and mold and death clung to them, they were actually greening forces, breathing life into seeds. They were described as tall, beautiful, dressed in green, and often invisible, so that only a ripple in the grass marked where they passed. A fuller discussion of the wood spirits can be found in *A Field Guide to the Little People* by Nancy Arrowsmith with George Moorse (New York: Farrar, Straus and Giroux, 1977; paperback reprint, New York: Simon & Schuster, 1978). In England, stories were told of a Green Lady, a wood spirit who protected a grove of trees, killing woodcutters. See "One Tree Hill" and other tales in *A Dictionary of British Folk-Tales in the English Language—Part A, Folk Narratives* by Katherine M. Briggs (New York and London: Routledge & Kegan Paul, 1970; paperback reprint, 1991).

A CAROLINA BANSHEE. Originally collected by J.C. Stutts for the Federal Writers' Project of the Works Progress Administration

232

(WPA) for the State of North Carolina in the 1930s. The WPA text is reprinted in *Ghost Stories of the American South* by W.K. McNeil (reissued with *Ghost Stories of the American Southwest* by Richard Alan Young and Judy Dockrey Young in a combined volume, *Ghastly Ghost Stories*, New Jersey: Wings Books, 1993). The story is unusual because the banshee (a Gaelic word meaning "supernatural woman") is traditionally an Irish spirit who foretells, but does not usually avenge, deaths. Stories alternately describe her as a lovely wraith or a hag with a sunken nose, scraggly white hair, huge, hollow eye sockets, and a tattered white sheet flapping about her. Her dismal wailing or singing always warns of someone's death. The "rain crow" is really a cuckoo, regarded as a herald of coming rain.

THE DEADLY VIOLIN. A retelling of a twelfth-century story from Germany. The original can be found translated in *Lilith's Cave: Jewish Tales of the Supernatural*, selected and retold by Howard Schwartz (New York: Harper & Row, 1998; paperback reprint Oxford and New York: Oxford University Press, 1991). I also consulted parallel tales of "haunted violins," which, along with fiddles, are well known in the folklore of Europe and America.

Music is often linked to mystical powers, and the violin is sometimes reported to have demonic characteristics. Related stories describe the Devil as a master fiddler, who will sometimes tempt fiddlers to sell their souls in order to master the instrument. In European folklore the fiddle is magic, variously causing fairies to dance, bringing the dead to life, summoning spirits or animals, or even revealing a murder.

A NIGHT OF TERRORS. A considerably reworked telling of the urban folktale "The Licked Hand"—widespread in America, Canada, great Britain, and Australia. A full discussion, with several examples, can be found in *The Choking Doberman: And Other "New" Urban Legends* by Jan Harold Brunvand (New York: W. W. Norton & Company, 1984). Variants include "The Licked Hand" in Hoosier Folk Legends by Ronald L. Baker (Bloomington: Indiana University Press, 1982) and "The Pet Dog" in *The Book of Nasty Legends* by Paul Smith (London, Boston, Melbourne and Henley: Routledge & Kegan Paul, 1983). Examples have also been found in European and Russian folklore.

THE SENDING. An expanded version of a traditional tale from Iceland, incorporating details from several accounts in *Legends of Icelandic Magicians*, edited and translated by Jacqueline Simpson (Cambridge: D.S. Brewer, Ltd., 1975; simultaneous publication in the U.S.A., Totowa, New Jersey: Rowman and Littlefield). The original can be found under the title "Murder by Spectral Proxy" in *The*

Enchanted World: Ghosts by the Editors of Time-Life Books (Alexandria, Virginia: Time-Life Books, Inc., 1984), and in *Icelandic Folktales and Legends* (Berkeley: University of California Press, 1979). The coming of Christianity caused the old Icelandic sorcerers to retreat to remote areas, where they continued to practice their magical arts. People would sometimes send for a white wizard to help with supernatural matters. In Scandinavian countries, trolls were powerful but stupid ogres who lurked in forests, mountains, and other wild areas. They would turn to stone or burst if the sun shone on their faces. Devils, demons, and imps often took the form of flies, and could be bottled up by a magician. This idea is the basis for such tales as "Aladdin and the Lamp" and Robert Louis Stevenson's "The Bottle Imp."

THE HAND OF FATE. Adapted from an account first published in England in the mid-seventeenth century. The full text is reprinted in *Sea Phantoms: True Tales of Haunted Ships and Ghostly Crews* by Warren Armstrong (London: Odhams Press, Limited, 1963). The land-based pirates called "wreckers" haunted the dangerous, desolate stretches of coast, plundering ships they lured onto the rocks and reefs. In the United States, in lonely coastal areas of New England, wreckers were called "mooncussers" or "moon cursers," because the light of a full moon would prevent ships from falling into their traps.

OLD RAW HEAD. Composited from various accounts of this favorite European and American bogey, including "Raw Head and Bloody Bones" in *Ghost Stories of the American Southwest*, compiled and edited by Richard Alan Young and Judy Dockrey Young (originally published by Little Rock: August House, 1991; reprinted with *Ghost Stories from the American South* in a combined edition titled *Ghastly Ghost Stories*, New Jersey: Wings Books, 1993); "Raw Head and Bloody Bones" in *Whistle in the Graveyard: Folktales to Chill Your Bones* by Maria Leach (New York: The Viking Press, Inc., 1974); and "High Walker and Bloody Bones: in *Mules and Men* by Zora Neale Hurston (Philadelphia and London: J.B. Lippincott Company, 1935); reprinted in *A Treasury of American Folklore*, edited by B.A. Botkin (New York: Crown Publishers, 1944). Written references to this horrifying creature go back as far as 1564; but scholars suggest the figure may have existed before in oral folklore. In England, Scotland, Canada, and the United States, adults would scare naughty children into obeying by telling them, "Raw Head and Bloody Bones will get you!" A version from Alabama makes it a "jump" story for campfire telling.

About the Author

Robert D. San Souci is the award-winning author of many books for young readers, including *Larger Than Life, Young Merlin, Young Guinevere, Feathertop, The Legend of Sleepy Hollow, Sootface,* and *The Hobyahs.* Widely traveled and a popular speaker, he has lectured in schools, libraries, universities, and conferences in more than thirty states. A native Californian, Robert San Souci lives in the San Francisco Bay Area.